"I hate a bossy woman."

"I can't stand crude men," Camilla retorted. "We'll both just have to live with it, since I'm currently washing your underwear."

The faintest glint of humor flicked into Del's eyes. "You've got plenty of starch. Just don't use any on my shorts."

They started for the door at the same time, and ended up jammed together. Camilla's hand went automatically to Del's chest, where she felt the surprised kick of his heart match hers.

"You're going to have to keep out of my way," Del told her.

"You'll have to watch where you're going, then." She saw, with reluctant excitement, his gaze lower, and linger on her mouth. In response, her lips parted on one quiet and catchy breath.

"You got that right, sister," Del muttered, and squeezed out of the door.

"Well." She breathed out, rubbing her finger experimentally over lips that felt just a little too warm. "Well, well."

Dear Reader,

Do I have a sweet lineup for you—just in time for Valentine's Day! What's more enticing than a box of chocolates? The answer lies in the next story, *Cordina's Crown Jewel*, from *New York Times* bestselling author Nora Roberts's CORDINA'S ROYAL FAMILY series. This gem features a princess who runs away from royal responsibility and straight into the arms of the most unlikely man of her dreams!

Another Valentine treat is Jackie Merritt's *Marked for Marriage*, which is part of the popular MONTANA MAVERICKS series. Here, a feisty bronco-busting beauty must sit still so that a handsome doctor can give her a healthy dose of love. And if it's heart-thumping emotion you want, Peggy Webb continues THE WESTMORELAND DIARIES series with *Bittersweet Passion*, a heavenly opposites-attract romance between a singing sensation and a very handsome minister hero.

In *With Family in Mind*, Sharon De Vita launches her gripping SADDLE FALLS miniseries. One Valentine's Day, this newlywed author admits, she wrote a heartwarming love poem to her husband about their first year together! Our next family tale is *Sun-Kissed Baby,* by Patricia Hagan—a darling tale of a new single mom who falls for the man she thinks is her little boy's father. This talented author shares her Valentine's Day dinner tradition with us—making "a heart-shaped meatloaf" and at the end of the pink meal, "a heart-shaped ice cream cake, frosted with strawberry whipped cream." The icing on the cake this month is Leigh Greenwood's *Undercover Honeymoon*, a passionate tale of two reunited lovers who join forces to stay ahead of a deadly enemy and care for an orphaned little girl.

Make sure that you sample every Special Edition delight this month has to offer. I wish you and your loved ones a warm and rose-filled Valentine's Day (and that box of chocolates, too)!

Best,

Karen Taylor Richman
Senior Editor

Please address questions and book requests to:
Silhouette Reader Service
U.S.: 3010 Walden Ave., P.O. Box 1325, Buffalo, NY 14269
Canadian: P.O. Box 609, Fort Erie, Ont. L2A 5X3

NORA ROBERTS

Cordina's Crown Jewel

SPECIAL EDITION™

Published by Silhouette Books

America's Publisher of Contemporary Romance

To all the new princes and princesses in my family.
May you all grow up strong and live happily ever after.

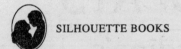 SILHOUETTE BOOKS

ISBN 0-373-24448-7

CORDINA'S CROWN JEWEL

Copyright © 2002 by Nora Roberts

This edition published by arrangement with Harlequin Books S.A.

® and TM are trademarks of Harlequin Books S.A., used under license.
Trademarks indicated with ® are registered in the United States Patent
and Trademark Office, the Canadian Trade Marks Office and in other
countries.

Visit Silhouette at www.eHarlequin.com

Printed in U.S.A.

Books by Nora Roberts

The MacGregors

The MacGregors: Serena~Caine
  containing *Playing the Odds* and
  Tempting Fate, Silhouette Books, 1998
The MacGregors: Alan~Grant
  containing *All the Possibilities* and
  One Man's Art, Silhouette Books, 1999
The MacGregors: Daniel~Ian
  containing *For Now, Forever* and
  In from the Cold, Silhouette Books, 1999
The MacGregor Brides,
  Silhouette Books, 1997
The Winning Hand SE #1202
The MacGregor Grooms,
  Silhouette Books, 1998
The Perfect Neighbor SE #1232
Rebellion, Harlequin Books, 1999

The O'Hurleys!

The Last Honest Woman SE #451
Dance to the Piper SE #463
Skin Deep SE #475
Without a Trace SE #625

The Calhoun Women

*The Calhoun Women: Catherine and
  Amanda* containing *Courting Catherine*
  and *A Man for Amanda*, Silhouette
  Books, 1998
The Calhoun Women: Lilah and Suzanna
  containing *For the Love of Lilah* and
  Suzanna's Surrender, Silhouette
  Books, 1998
Megan's Mate IM #745

The Stars of Mithra

Hidden Star IM #811
Captive Star IM #823
Secret Star IM #835

The Donovan Legacy

The Donovan Legacy
  containing *Captivated, Entranced* and
  Charmed, Silhouette Books, 1999
Enchanted IM #961

Cordina's Royal Family

Cordina's Royal Family
  containing *Affaire Royale,
  Command Performance* and
  The Playboy Prince,
  Silhouette Books, 2002
Cordina's Crown Jewel SE #1448

The Stanislaskis

*The Stanislaski Brothers:
  Mikhail and Alex*,
  Silhouette Books, 2000
*The Stanislaski Sisters:
  Natasha and Rachel*,
  Silhouette Books, 2001
Waiting for Nick SE #1088
Considering Kate SE #1379
Reflections and Dreams containing
  Reflections and *Dance of Dreams*,
  Silhouette Books, 2000

Night Tales

Night Tales containing
  *Night Shift
  Night Shadow
  Nightshade*
  and *Night Smoke*,
  Silhouette Books, 2000
Night Shield IM #1027

The MacKade Brothers

*The Return of
  Rafe MacKade* IM #631
*The Pride of
  Jared MacKade* SE #1000
*The Heart of
  Devin MacKade* IM #697
*The Fall of
  Shane MacKade* SE #1022

Silhouette Books

Silhouette Christmas Stories 1986
"Home for Christmas"

Silhouette Summer Sizzlers 1989
"Impulse"

Birds, Bees and Babies 1994
"The Best Mistake"

Jingle Bells, Wedding Bells 1994
"All I Want for Christmas"

Irish Hearts

Irish Hearts containing
  Irish Thoroughbred, and
  Irish Rose, Silhouette Books, 2000
Irish Rebel SE #1328

Time and Again containing
  Time Was, and *Times Change*,
  Silhouette Books, 2001

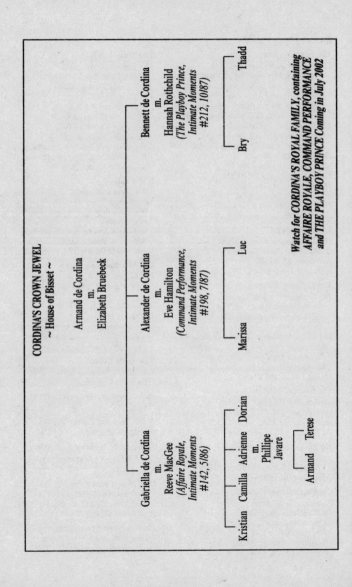

CORDINA'S CROWN JEWEL
~ House of Bisset ~

Armand de Cordina
m.
Elizabeth Bruebeck

Gabriella de Cordina
m.
Reeve MacGee
*(Affaire Royale,
Intimate Moments
#142, 5/86)*

Kristian Camilla Adrienne Dorian
m.
Phillippe
Javare

Armand Terese

Alexander de Cordina
m.
Eve Hamilton
*(Command Performance,
Intimate Moments
#198, 7/87)*

Marissa Luc

Bennett de Cordina
m.
Hannah Rothchild
*(The Playboy Prince,
Intimate Moments
#212, 10/87)*

Bry Thadd

*Watch for CORDINA'S ROYAL FAMILY, containing
AFFAIRE ROYALE, COMMAND PERFORMANCE
and THE PLAYBOY PRINCE Coming in July 2002*

Prologue

She was a princess. Born, bred and meticulously trained. Her deportment was flawless, her speech impeccable and her manners unimpeachable. The image she presented was one of youth, confidence and grace all wrapped up in a lovely and carefully polished package.

Such things, she knew, were expected of a member of Cordina's royal family—at least in the public arena. The charity gala in Washington, D.C. was a very public arena. So she did her duty, greeting guests who had paid handsomely for the opportunity to rub elbows with royalty.

She watched her mother, Her Serene Highness Gabriella de Cordina, glide effortlessly through the process. At least her mother made it seem effortless, though she had worked as brutally hard as her daughter on this event.

She saw her father—so wonderfully handsome and steady—and her eldest brother who was serving as her escort for the evening, mingle smoothly with the crowd. A crowd that included politicians, celebrities and the very wealthy.

When it was time, Her Royal Highness Camilla de Cordina took her seat for the first portion of the evening's entertainment. Her hair was dressed in a complicated twist that left her slender neck bare, but for the glitter of emeralds. Her dress was an elegant black that was designed to accent her willowy frame. A frame both she and her dressmaker knew was in danger of slipping to downright thin.

Her appetite was not what it had been.

Her face was composed, her posture perfect. A headache raged like a firestorm behind her eyes.

She was a princess, but she was also a woman on the edge.

She applauded. She smiled. She laughed.

It was nearly midnight—eighteen hours into her official day—when her mother managed a private word by sliding an arm around Camilla's waist and dipping her head close.

"Darling, you don't look well." It took a mother's sharp eyes to see the exhaustion, and Gabriella's eyes were sharp indeed.

"I'm a bit tired, that's all."

"Go. Go back to the hotel. Don't argue," she murmured. "You've been working too hard, much too hard. I should have insisted you take a few weeks at the farm."

"There's been so much to do."

"And you've done enough. I've already told Marian to alert security and see to your car. Your father and I will be leaving within the hour ourselves.'' Gabriella glanced over, noted her son was entertaining—and being entertained by—a popular American singer. "Do you want Kristian with you?"

"No." It was a sign of her fatigue that she didn't argue. "No, he's enjoying himself. Wiser to slip out separately anyway." And quietly, she hoped.

"The Americans love you, perhaps a little too much." With a smile, Gabriella kissed her daughter's cheek. "Go, get some rest. We'll talk in the morning."

But it was not to be a quiet escape. Despite the decoy car, the security precautions, the tedium of winding through the building to a side entrance, the press had scented her.

She had no more than stepped out into the night when she was blinded by the flash of cameras. The shouts rained over her, pounded in her head. She sensed the surge of movement, felt the tug of hands and was appalled to feel her legs tremble as her bodyguards rushed her to the waiting limo.

Unable to see, to think, she fought to maintain her composure as she was swept through the stampede, bodyguards pressed on either side of her rushing her forward.

It was so horribly hot, so horribly close. Surely that was why she felt ill. Ill and weak and stupidly frightened. She wasn't sure if she fell, was pushed or simply dived in to the car.

As the door slammed behind her, and the shouts were like the roar of the sea outside the steel and glass, she shivered, her teeth almost chattering in the sudden wash of cool air-conditioned air. Closed her eyes.

"Your Highness, are you all right?"

She heard, dimly, the concerned voice of one of her guards. "Yes. Thank you, yes. I'm fine."

But she knew she wasn't.

Chapter One

Whatever might, and undoubtedly would be said, it hadn't been an impulsive decision. Her Royal Highness Camilla de Cordina was not an impulsive woman.

She was, however, a desperate one.

Desperation, she was forced to admit, had been building in her for months. On this hot, sticky, endless June night, it had reached, despite her efforts to deny it, a fever pitch.

The wild hive of paparazzi that had swarmed after her when she'd tried to slip out of the charity gala that evening had been the final straw.

Even as security had worked to block them, as she'd managed to slide into her limo with some remnants of dignity, her mind had been screaming.

Let me breathe. For pity's sake, give me some space.

Now, two hours later, temper, excitement, nerves and frustration continued to swirl around her as she paced the floor of the sumptuous suite high over Washington, D.C.

Less than three hours to the south was the farm where she'd spent part of her childhood. Several thousand miles east across the ocean was the tiny country where she'd spent the other part. Her life had been divided between those two worlds. Though she loved both equally, she wondered if she would ever find her own place in either.

It was time, past time, she found it somewhere.

To do that, she had to find herself first. And how could she do that when she was forever surrounded. Worse, she thought, when she was beginning to feel continually hounded. Perhaps if she hadn't been the eldest of the three young women of the new generation of Cordinian princesses—and for the past few years the most accessible due to her American father and time spent in the States—it would have been different.

But she was, so it wasn't. Just now, it seemed her entire existence was bound up in politics, protocol and press. Requests, demands, appointments, obligations. She'd completed her duty as co-chair for the Aid To Children with Disabilities benefit—a task she'd shared with her mother.

She believed in what she was doing, knew the duty was required, important. But did the price have to be so high?

It had taken weeks of organizing and effort, and the pleasure of seeing all that work bear fruit had been spoiled by her own bone-deep weariness.

How they crowded her, she thought. All those cameras, all those faces.

Even her family, God love them, seemed to crowd her too much these days. Trying to explain her feelings to her personal assistant seemed disloyal, ungrateful and impossible. But the assistant was also her oldest and dearest friend.

"I'm sick of seeing my face on the cover of magazines, of reading about my supposed romances inside them. Marian, I'm just so tired of having other people define me."

"Royalty, beauty and sex sell magazines. Combine the three and you can't print them fast enough." Marian Breen was a practical woman, and her tone reflected that. As she'd known Camilla since childhood it also reflected more amusement than respect. "I know tonight was horrid, and I don't blame you for being shaken by it. If we find out who leaked your exit route—"

"It's done. What does it matter who?"

"They were like a pack of hounds," Marian muttered. "Still, you're a princess of Cordina—a place that makes Americans in particular think of fairy tales. You look like your mother, which means you're stunning. And you attract men like an out of business sale attracts bargain hunters. The press, particularly the more aggressive element, feed on that."

"The royalty is a product of birth, as are my looks. As for the men—" Camilla dismissed the entire gender with an imperious flick of the wrist. "None of them are attracted to *me* but to the package—the same one that sells the idiotic magazines in the first place."

"Catch-22." Since Camilla was keeping her up, Marian nibbled on the grapes from the impressive fruit bowl that had been sent up by the hotel management. Outwardly calm, inwardly she was worried. Her friend was far too pale. And she looked like she'd lost weight.

It was nothing, she assured herself, that a few quiet days in Virginia wouldn't put right. The farm was as secure as the palace in Cordina. Camilla's father had made certain of it.

"I know it's a pain to have bodyguards and paparazzi surrounding you every time you take a step in public," she continued. "But what're you going to do? Run away from home?"

"Yes."

Chuckling, Marian plucked another grape. Then it spurted out of her fingers as she caught the steely gleam in Camilla's tawny eyes. "Obviously you had too much champagne at the benefit."

"I had one glass," Camilla said evenly. "And I didn't even finish it."

"It must've been some glass. Listen, I'm going back to my room like a good girl, and I'm going to let you sleep off this mood."

"I've been thinking about it for weeks." Toying with the idea, she admitted. Fantasizing about it. Tonight, she was going to make it happen. "I need your help, Marian."

"Non, non, c'est impossible. C'est completement fou!"

Marian rarely slid into French. She was, at the core, American as apple pie. Her parents had settled in Cordina when she'd been ten—and she and Camilla had been fast friends ever since. A small woman with her honey-brown hair still upswept from the evening, she responded in the language of her adopted country as she began to panic. Her eyes, a warm, soft blue, were wide with alarm.

She knew the look on her friend's face. And feared it.

"It's neither impossible nor crazy," Camilla responded easily. "It's both possible and sane. I need time, a few weeks. And I'm going to take them. As Camilla MacGee, not as Camilla de Cordina. I've lived with the title almost without rest since Grand-père…"

She trailed off. It hurt, still. Nearly four years since his death and it still grieved inside her.

"He was our rock," she continued, drawing together her composure. "Even though he'd passed so much of the control already to his son, to Uncle Alex, he still ruled. Since his death, the family's had to contribute more—to pull together. I wouldn't have wanted it otherwise. I've been happy to do more in an official capacity."

"But?" Resigned now, Marian lowered herself to perch on the arm of the sofa.

"I need to get away from the hunt. That's how I feel," Camilla said, pressing a hand to her heart. "Hunted. I can't step out on the street without photographers dogging me. I'm losing myself in it. I don't know what I am anymore. There are times, too many times now, I can't *feel* me anymore."

"You need a rest. You need a break."

"Yes, but it's more. It's more complicated than that. Marian, I don't know what I want, for me. For myself. Look at Adrienne," she continued, speaking of her younger sister. "Married at twenty-one. She set eyes on Phillipe when she was six, and that was that. She knew what she wanted—to marry him, to raise pretty babies in Cordina. My brothers are like two halves of my father. One the farmer, one the security expert. I have no direction, Marian. No skills.''

"That's not true. You were brilliant in school. Your mind's like a damn computer when you find something that sparks it. You're a spectacular hostess, you work tirelessly for worthwhile causes.''

"Duties," Camilla murmured. "I excel at them. And for pleasure? I can play piano, sing a little. Paint a little, fence a little. Where's my passion?'' She crossed her hands between her breasts. "I'm going to find it—or at least spend a few weeks without the bodyguards, without the protocol, without the damn press—*trying* to find it. If I don't get away from the press," she said quietly. "I'm afraid—very afraid— I'll just break into pieces.''

"Talk to your parents, Cam. They'd understand.''

"Mama would. I'm not sure about Daddy.'' But she smiled as she said it. "Adrienne's been married three years, and he still hasn't gotten over losing his baby. And Mama…she was my age when she married. Another one who knew what she wanted. But before that…''

She shook her head as she began to pace again. "The kidnapping, and the assassination attempts on my family. Passages in history books now, but still very real and immediate for us. I can't blame my parents for sheltering their children. I'd have done the same. But I'm not a child anymore, and I need… something of my own.''

"A holiday then.''

"No, a quest.'' She moved to Marian, took her hands. "You rented a car.''

"Yes, I needed to—oh. Oh, Camilla.''

"Give me the keys. You can call the agency and extend the rental."

"You can't just drive out of Washington."

"I'm a very good driver."

"Think! You drop out of sight, your family will go mad. And the press."

"I'd never let my family worry. I'll call my parents first thing in the morning. And the press will be told I'm taking that holiday—in an undisclosed location. You'll leak Europe, so they'll hardly be hunting around for me in the U.S."

"Shall I point out that what started this madness was you being annoyed by having your face splashed all over magazines?" Marian plucked one from the coffee table, held it up. "You have one of the most famous images in the world, Cam. You don't blend."

"I will." Though she knew it was foolish, Camilla's stomach jumped as she walked to the desk, pulled open a drawer. And removed a pair of scissors. "Princess Camilla." She shook her waist-length fall of dark red hair, and sucked in her breath. "Is about it get a whole new look."

Horror, so huge it would've been comical if Camilla hadn't felt an echo of it inside herself, spread over Marian's face. "You don't mean it! Camilla, you can't just—just whack off your hair. Your beautiful hair."

"You're right." Camilla held out the scissors. "You do it."

"Me? Oh no—absolutely not." Instantly Marian whipped her hands behind her back. "What we're going to do is sit down, have a nice glass of wine and wait for this insanity to pass. You'll feel better tomorrow."

Camilla was afraid of that. Afraid it would pass and she'd go on just as she was. Doing her duty, fulfilling her obligations, sliding back into the bright lights and the undeniable comfort of her life. The unbearable fleeing from the media.

If she didn't do something—*something*—now, would she ever? Or would she, as the media continued to predict, marry one of the glossy men deemed suitable for someone in her position and rank and just...go on.

She set her jaw, lifted it in a way that made her friend gasp. And taking a long lock of hair, snipped it off.

"Oh, God!" Weak at the knees, Marian folded herself into a chair. "Oh, Camilla."

"It's just hair." But her hand trembled a little. Her hair had become so much a part of her image, of her life, that one snip was like cutting off a hand. She stared at the long length of gilded red that dangled from her fingers. "I'm going in the bathroom to do the rest. I could use some help with the back."

In the end, Marian came through, as friends do. By the time they were finished, the floor was littered with hanks of hair and Camilla's vision of herself with long flowing hair had to be completely adjusted. A snip here, a snip there. A glass of wine for fortification. Another snip to even things up. And she'd ended up with a cap short as a boy's, with long spiky bangs to balance it out.

"It's awfully—well...different," Camilla managed to say.

"I'm going to cry."

"No, you're not." And neither, Camilla vowed,

was she. "I need to change, and pack some things. I'm already behind schedule."

She packed what she felt were essentials and was both surprised and a bit ashamed that they filled a suitcase and a enormous tote to bursting. She put on jeans, boots, a sweater and topped them all with a long black coat.

She considered sunglasses and a hat, but decided the addition would make her *look* like she was in disguise rather than letting her pass unnoticed.

"How do I look?" she demanded.

"Not like you." Marian shook her head and walked two slow circles around Camilla.

The short hair was a dramatic change, and to Marian's surprise an intriguing one. It made Camilla's golden-brown eyes seem bigger and somehow more vulnerable. The bangs concealed the regal forehead and added a youthful edge. Without makeup, her face was rose and cream, maybe a bit paler than it should be. The high cheekbones stood out, and the long mouth seemed fuller.

Rather than cool, aloof and elegant, she looked young, careless and just a little reckless.

"Not like you at all," Marian said again. "I'd recognize you, but it would take me a minute, and a second look."

"That's good enough." She checked her watch. "If I leave now I can be well away before morning."

"Camilla, where are you going to go?"

"Anywhere." She took her friend by the shoulders, kissed both Marian's cheeks. "Don't worry about me. I'll keep in touch. I promise. Even a princess is entitled to a little adventure." Her long mouth bowed up in a smile. "Maybe *especially* a princess. Promise me you won't say anything to anyone before eight in the morning—and then only to my family.''

"I don't like it, but I promise.''

"Thanks.'' She hefted the tote then walked over to pick up the suitcase.

"Wait. Don't walk like that.''

Baffled, Camilla turned back. "Like what?''

"Like a princess. Slouch a little, swing your hips a little. I don't know, Cam, walk like a girl. Don't glide.''

"Oh." Adjusting the strap of the tote, she practiced. "Like this?''

"Better.'' Marian tapped a finger on her lips. "Try taking the steel rod out of your backbone.''

She worked on it a bit, trying for a looser, easier gait. "I'll practice,'' she promised. "But I have to go now. I'll call in the morning.''

Marian rushed after her as Camilla headed for the bedroom door. "Oh, God. Be careful. Don't talk to strangers. Lock the car doors. Um... Do you have money, your phone? Have you—''

"Don't worry.'' At the door, Camilla turned, shot out one brilliant smile. "I have everything I need. *A bientôt.*''

But when the door shut behind her, Marian wrung her hands. "Oh boy. *Bonne chance, m'amie.*''

After ten days, Camilla sang along with the radio. She *loved* American music. She loved driving. She loved doing and going exactly what and where she wanted. Not that the interlude had been without its snags. She knew her parents were concerned. Especially her father, she mused.

There was too much cop in him, she supposed, for

him not to imagine every possible pitfall and disaster that could befall a young woman alone. Especially when the young woman was his daughter.

He'd insisted she call every day. She'd been firm on offering a once-a-week check-in. And her mother—as always the balance—had negotiated between the two for every three days.

She loved them so much. Loved what they were to her, to each other. What they were to the world. But it was so much to live up to. And, she knew, they would be appalled that she felt so strongly she had to live up to anything, anyone, but herself.

Other snags were more practical than emotional. It had struck her the first time she'd checked into a motel—and what an experience that had been—that she couldn't risk using a credit card. If any clever clerk tagged the name Camilla MacGee and realized who she was, with one call to the local papers she would be—as her brother Dorian would say—busted.

As a result, her cash was dwindling quickly. Pride, stubbornness and sheer annoyance at her own lack of foresight prevented her from asking her parents to front her the means to continue with her journey.

It would, after all, negate one of the purposes. A few precious weeks of total independence.

She wondered how one went about pawning an item. Her watch was worth several thousand dollars. That would be more than enough to see her through. Perhaps she'd look into it at her next stop.

But for now it was glorious to simply drive. She'd headed north and west from Washington, and had enjoyed exploring parts of West Virginia and Pennsylvania.

She'd eaten in fast-food restaurants, slept in lumpy

beds in highway motels. She'd strolled the streets of
small towns and larger cities, had been jostled rudely
in crowds. And once had been ignored, then snapped
at by a convenience store clerk when she'd stopped
for a soft drink.

It had been marvelous.

No one—absolutely no one—had taken her picture.

When she'd wandered through a little park in up-
state New York, she'd seen two old men playing
chess. She stopped to watch, and found herself being
drawn in to their discussion of world politics. It had
been both fascinating and delightful.

She'd loved watching summer burst over New England. It was all so different from her homes in Cordina and Virginia. It was all so…liberating to simply
drift where no one knew her, where no one expected
anything of her, or caught her between the crosshairs
of a camera lens.

She found herself doing something she did only
with family, and the most intimate of friends. Relax-
ing.

Each night, for her own pleasure, she recounted the
day's events and her observations in a journal.

Very tired now, but pleasantly so, she'd written
last. *Tomorrow I'll cross into Vermont. From there I
must decide whether to continue east to the coast, or
turn. America is so big. None of the books, the lessons, none of the trips I've taken with family or on
official business had really shown me the size, the
diversity, the extraordinary beauty of the country itself, or the people in it.*

*I'm half American, have always found pride in that
part of my heritage. Oddly, the longer I'm on my own*

*here, the more foreign I feel. I have, I see, neglected
this part of my blood. But no more.*

*I'm in a small motel off the interstate, in the Adi-
rondack Mountains. They are spectacular. I can't ap-
ply the same description to my room. It's clean, but
very cramped. Amenities run to a cake of soap the
size of a U.S. quarter and two towels rough as sand-
paper. But there's a soft drink machine just outside
my door should I want one.*

*I'd love a good glass of wine, but my budget
doesn't run to such luxuries just now.*

*I called home this evening. Mama and Daddy are
in Virginia at the farm, as are Kristian and Dorian.
I miss them, the comfort and reliability they represent.
But I'm so happy I'm finding out who I am and that
I can be alone.*

*I believe I'm fairly self-sufficient, and more daring
than I'd imagined. I have a good eye for detail, an
excellent sense of direction and am easier in my own
company than I thought I might be.*

*I have no idea what any of this means in the grand
scheme, but it's all very nice to know.*

*Perhaps, if the bottom drops out of the princess
market, I could get work as a trail guide.*

She adored Vermont. She loved the high green
mountains, the many lakes, the winding rivers. Rather
than cut through toward Maine, or turn west, back
into New York state, she took a rambling route
through the state, leaving the interstate for roads
through tidy New England towns, through forest and
farmland.

She forgot about trying to sell her watch and put
off scouting out a motel. She had the windows open

to the warm summer air, the radio up, and munched on the fast-food fries in the bag tucked in her lap.

It didn't concern her when the sky clouded over. It added such an interesting light to the tall trees lining the road, and gave the air blowing in her windows a faint electric edge.

She didn't particularly mind when rain began to splatter the windshield, though it meant winding up the windows or getting soaked. And when lightning slashed over the sky, she enjoyed the show.

But when the rain began to pound, the wind to howl and those lights in the sky became blinding, she decided it was time to make her way back to the interstate and find shelter.

Ten minutes later, she was cursing herself and struggling to see the road through the curtain of rain the windshield wipers washed rapidly from side to side.

Her own fault, she thought grimly. She was now driving into the teeth of the storm rather than away from it. And she was afraid in the dark, in the driving rain, she'd missed—or would miss her turn.

She could see nothing but the dark gleam of asphalt, pierced by her own headlights, the thick wall of trees on either side. Thunder blasted, and the wind rocked the car under her.

She considered pulling over waiting it out. But the stubborn streak—the one her brothers loved to tease her about—pushed her on. Just a couple more miles, she told herself. She'd be back on the main road. Then she'd find a motel and be inside, safe and dry, and be able to enjoy the storm.

Something streaked out of the trees and leaped in front of the car. She had an instant to see the deer's eyes gleam in her headlights, another to jerk the wheel.

The car fishtailed, spun in a complete circle on the slick road, and ended up—with a jolt and an ominous squeal of metal—front-first in a ditch.

For the next few minutes, there was no sound but the hard drum of rain and her own ragged breathing. Then a flash of lightning slapped her clear of shock.

She drew in breath slowly, released it again. Repeating this three times usually served to calm her. But this time that third breath came out with an oath. She slapped the wheel, gritted her teeth, then slammed the car in reverse.

When she hit the gas, her wheels spun and dug their way deeper. She tried rocking the car—forward, reverse, forward, reverse. For every inch she gained, she lost two.

Giving up, muttering insults at herself, she climbed out in the pouring rain to take stock.

She couldn't see any body damage beyond a scraped fender—but it was dark. Darker yet, she noted, as one of her headlights was smashed. The car was not only half on, half off the road, but the front tires were sunk deep.

Shivering now as the rain soaked through her shirt, she climbed back into the car and dug out her cell phone. She'd need to call a tow truck, and hadn't a clue how to go about it. But she imagined the operator would be able to connect her.

Camilla turned on the phone, then stared at the display. *No Service.*

Perfect, she thought in disgust. Just perfect. I drive into the middle of nowhere because the trees are pretty, sing my way into a vicious summer storm, and end up getting run off the road and into a ditch by an idiotic deer in the one place in the world where there's no damn mobile phone service.

It appeared the next part of her adventure would be to spend the night, soaking wet, in her car.

After ten minutes, the discomfort sent her back into the rain and around to the trunk for her suitcase.

Next adventure: changing into dry clothes in a car on the side of the road.

As she started to drag the case out, she caught the faint gleam of headlights piercing through the rain. She didn't hesitate, but rushed back around to the driver's side, reached in and blasted the horn three times. She slipped, nearly ended up facedown in the ditch, then scrambled back up to the road where she waved her arms frantically.

No white charger had ever looked as magnificent as the battered truck that rumbled up, and eased to a stop beside her. No knight in shining armor had ever looked as heroic as the dark figure who rolled down the window and stared out at her.

She couldn't see the color of his eyes, or even gauge his age in the poor light and drenching rain. She saw only the vague shape of his face, a tousled head of hair as she ran over.

"I had some trouble," she began.

"No kidding."

She saw his eyes now—they were green as glass, and sharply annoyed under dark brows that were knitted together in a scowl. They passed over her as if she were a minor inconvenience—a fact that had her hackles rising even as she struggled to be grateful—and studied the car.

"You should've pulled *onto* the shoulder during a storm like this,'' he shouted over the wind, "not driven your car off it.''

"That's certainly helpful advice.'' Her tone went frigid, and horribly polite—a skill that had goaded her brothers into dubbing her Princess Prissy.

His eyes flicked back to her with a gleam that might have been humor. Or temper. "I'd very much appreciate it if you'd help me get it back on the road.''

"Bet you would.'' His voice was deep, rough and just a little weary. "But since I left my super power suit on Krypton, I'm afraid you're out of luck.''

She sent him one long stare. He had a strong face, she could see that now. It was raw boned and shadowed by what seemed to be two or three days' worth of beard. His mouth was hard and set in stern lines. Professorial lines, she thought. The kind that might just lecture.

She was hardly in the mood.

She fought off a shudder from the chill, fought to maintain her dignity. "There must be something that can be done.''

"Yeah.'' His sigh told her he wasn't too happy about it. "Get in. We'll go to my place, call for a tow.''

In the car? With him?

Don't talk to strangers.

Marian's warning echoed in her ears. Of course, she'd ignored that advice a dozen times over the last week and a half. But get into the car with one, on a deserted road?

Still, if he'd meant her harm, he didn't need her to get into the car. He could simply climb out, bash her on the head and be done with it.

So, faced with spending hours in her disabled car or taking a chance on him and finding a dry spot and—God willing—hot coffee, she nodded. "My bags are in the trunk," she told him.

"Fine. Go get them."

At this, she blinked. Then, when he simply continued to scowl at her, set her teeth.

Shining knight her butt, she fumed as she trudged through the rain to retrieve her bags. He was a rude, miserable, ill-mannered boor.

But if he had a telephone and a coffeepot, she could overlook it.

She heaved her bags in the back then climbed in beside him.

It was then she saw that his right arm was in a sling strapped close to his body. Immediately guilt swamped her.

Naturally he couldn't help with the car, or her bags, if he was injured. And he was likely impolite due to discomfort. To make up for her hard thoughts, she sent him a brilliant smile.

"Thanks so much for helping me. I was afraid I'd have to spend the night in the car—soaking wet."

"Wouldn't be wet if you'd stayed in the car."

Something wanted to hiss out between her teeth, but she swallowed it. Diplomacy, even when it wasn't deserved, was part of her training. "True. Still, I appreciate you stopping, Mr...."

"Caine. Delaney Caine."

"Mr. Caine." She pushed at her wet hair as he drove through the storm. "I'm Camilla—" She broke off, the briefest of hesitations when she realized she'd been about to say MacGee. The episode had rattled her more than she'd realized. "Breen," she finished, giving Marian's last name as her own. "How did you hurt your arm?"

"Look, let's just ditch the small talk." He was driving, one handed, through a wailing bitch of a storm, and the woman wanted to chat. Amazing. "We both just want to get out of the rain, and put you back on the road to wherever the hell you're going."

Make that ill-mannered swine, she decided. "Very well." She turned her head and stared out the side window.

One advantage, she decided. The man hadn't looked at her twice—had barely managed once. She wouldn't have to worry about him identifying the damsel in distress as a princess.

Chapter Two

Oh, he'd looked at her all right.

It might have been dark, she might have been wet and spitting mad. But that kind of beauty managed to punch through every obstacle.

He'd seen a long, slender, soaked woman in shirt and jeans that had clung to every subtle curve. He'd seen a pale oval face dominated by gold eyes and a wide, mobile mouth and crowned by a sleek cap of hair that was dark fire with rain.

He'd heard a voice that hinted of the South and of France simultaneously. It was a classy, cultured combination that whispered upper crust.

He'd noticed the slight hesitation over her name, and had known she lied. He just didn't happen to give a damn about that, or any of the rest of it.

She was, at the moment, no more than a nuisance. He wanted to get home. To be alone. To pop some of the medication that would ease the throbbing of his shoulder and ribs. The damp and the rain were killing him.

He had work to do, damn it, and dealing with her was likely to cut a good hour out of his evening schedule.

On top of it all, she'd actually wanted to chatter at him. What was it with people and their constant need to hear voices? Particularly their own.

The one benefit of having to leave the dig in Florida and recover at home was being home. Alone. No amateurs trying to horn in on the site, no students battering him with questions, no press wheedling for an interview.

Of course, the downside was he hadn't realized how problematic it would be to try to deal with paperwork, with cataloging, with every damn thing essentially one-handed.

But he was managing.

Mostly.

It was just an hour or so, he reminded himself. He couldn't have left the woman stranded on the side of the road in the middle of a storm. Okay, he'd considered it—but only for a couple seconds. A minute, max.

Brooding, he didn't notice her shivering on the seat beside him. But he did notice when she huffed irritably and leaned over to turn up the heat.

He only grunted and kept driving.

Baboon, Camilla thought. Delany Caine was rapidly descending the evolutionary chain in her mind. When he turned into a narrow, rain-rutted, bone-jarring lane that had her bouncing on the seat, she decided he didn't deserve whole mammal status and regulated him to horse's ass.

Cold, miserable, fuming, she tried to make out the shape of the structure ahead of them. It was nestled in the woods, and looked to be some sort of cabin. She assumed it was wood—it was certainly dark. She caught a glimpse of an overgrown lawn and a sagging front porch as he muscled the truck around what was hardly more than a mud-packed path to the back of the building.

There, a yellow, unshielded lightbulb was burning beside a door.

"You...live here?"

"Sometimes." He shoved open his door. "Grab what you need, leave the rest." And with that, he stomped through the rain toward the back door.

Since she needed, more than breath, to change into dry, warm clothes, Camilla dragged her cases out and lugged them toward the cabin. She had to maneuver to open the door, as he hadn't bothered to wait for her or hold it open as any Neanderthal with even half a pea for a brain would have.

Out of breath, she shoved through into a tiny mud-room that lived up to its name. It was, in a word, filthy—as was everything in it. Boots, coats, hats, gloves, buckets, small shovels. Under a heap of pails, trowels and laundry were, she assumed, a small washer and dryer unit.

Cochon, she thought. The man was a complete pig.

The opinion wasn't swayed when she walked through and into the kitchen. The sink was full of dishes, the small table covered with more. Along with papers, a pair of glasses, an open bag of cookies and several pencil stubs.

Her feet stuck to the floor and made little sucking sounds as she walked.

"I see soap and water are rare commodities in Vermont."

She said it sweetly with a polite smile. He only shrugged. "I fired the cleaning lady. Wouldn't leave my stuff alone."

"How, I wonder, could she find it under the dirt?"

"Tow truck," he muttered, and dug out an ancient phone book.

At least he seemed to be fairly clean, Camilla mused. That was something at least. He was roughly dressed, and his boots were scarred, but his hands and hair—though it was long, wet and unkempt—were clean. She thought his face might even be handsome—of a type—under that untidy beard.

It was a hard face, and somewhat remote, but the eyes were striking. And looked fairly intelligent.

She waited, with admirable patience, she thought, while he found the number. Then he picked up the phone, started to punch in a button. Swore.

"Phone's out."

No, she thought, fate couldn't be so cruel. "Are you sure?"

"On this planet, no dial tone equals no phone."

They stared at each other with equal levels of dismay and annoyance. Her teeth wanted to chatter.

"Perhaps you could drive me to the nearest inn, or motel."

He glanced toward the window as the next blast of lightning lit the glass. "Twenty miles in this—flash flooding, high winds." He rubbed his aching shoulder absently. Two good arms, he might have tried it, just to get rid of her. But with one, it wasn't worth it. "I don't think so."

"What would you suggest?"

"I'd suggest you get on some dry clothes before you end up sick—which would just cap things for me here. Then we'll see if we can find something to eat in this place, and make the best of it."

"Mr. Caine, that is incredibly gracious of you. But I wouldn't want to—" She sneezed, three times in rapid succession.

"Down the hall," he told her, pointing. "Up the stairs. Bathroom's all the way at the end. I'll make coffee."

Too chilled to argue or think of an alternative, she picked up her suitcases again, struggled with them down the short hall and up the stairs. Like a horse with blinders heading toward the finish line, she kept her gaze straight ahead and closed herself in the bathroom.

Locked the door.

There were towels on the floor, toothpaste—sans cap—on the counter on a small white sink that, while not gleaming, at least appeared to have been rinsed sometime within the last six months.

There was also, she soon discovered, hot water.

The minute she stepped into the shower, the glory of it wiped out every other sensation. She let it beat on her, flood over her head. She very nearly danced in it. When the warmth reached her bones, she simply closed her eyes and sighed.

It was with some regret that she turned off the taps, stepped out. Locating a reasonably clean-looking towel on the rack, she wrapped herself in it as she dug out a shirt and trousers.

She was standing in her underwear when the lights went out.

She screamed. She couldn't help it, and ended up ramming her hip sharply against the sink before she controlled herself.

Her hands shook and her temper spiked as she fought to dress herself in the dark.

"Mr. Caine!" she shouted for him as she inched out of the bath. The place was pitch-black.

"Yeah, yeah, don't blow a gasket."

She heard him tromping up the stairs, saw the narrow beam of light bobbing with him. "Power's out," he told her.

"I never would've guessed."

"Perfect time for sarcasm," he muttered. "Just stay put." He and the light disappeared into another room. He came back with the flashlight, and offered her a flickering candle. "You done in there?" he gestured with his head toward the bathroom.

"Yes, thank you."

"Fine." He started back down, and the next boom of thunder had her hurrying after him.

"What do we do now?"

"We build a fire, drink coffee, heat up some soup and wish you were someplace else."

"I don't see any reason to be rude. It's hardly my fault there's a storm." She tripped over a pair of shoes and rapped into his back.

"Damn it!" The jar had his shoulder singing. "Watch it, will you?"

"I beg your pardon. If you didn't live like a pig, I wouldn't trip over your mess."

"Look, just go in there." He pointed to the front room of the cabin. "Sit down. Stay out of the way."

"Gladly." She sailed into the room, then spoiled the effect by letting out a muffled shriek. "Are those..." She lifted a hand weakly toward what her light had picked out on a littered table. "Bones?"

Del shined the flashlight over the bones sealed in airtight plastic. "Yeah. Human, mostly." He said it matter-of-factly as he headed toward the fireplace. "Don't worry." He crouched and set kindling. "I didn't kill anyone."

"Oh, really." She was edging back, wondering what she might use for a weapon.

"The original owner died about seven thousand years ago—but not in the fall that fractured a number of those bones. Anyway, she doesn't miss them." He set the kindling to light.

"Why do you have them?"

"I found them—on a dig in Florida."

He set logs to blaze and stood. The fire snapped at his back, shooting light around him. "You...dig graves?" she managed to ask, the horror only a hint in her voice.

For the first time, he smiled. It was a flash as bright as the lightning that shot across the sky. "In a manner of speaking. Relax...what was your name?"

She moistened her lips. "Camilla."

"Right, well relax, Camilla. I'm an archaeologist, not a mad scientist. I'm going for the coffee. Don't touch my bones—or anything else for that matter."

"I wouldn't dream of it." She also wouldn't dream of staying alone in the dark room on a storm ravaged night with a pile of human bones. No matter how carefully packaged or old they might be. "I'll give you a hand." Because she wanted to cover her unease, she smiled. "You look like you could use one."

"Yeah, I guess." The injury still irritated him, in more ways than one. "Look, there's a spare room upstairs. You might as well figure on bunking there. We'll deal with your car in the morning."

"Thanks." She was warm, she was dry and the coffee smelled wonderful. Things might've been a great deal worse. "I really do appreciate it, Mr. Caine."

"Caine, just Caine, or Del." When he walked straight back to the mudroom, she followed him.

"Where are you going?"

"What?" He paused in the act of struggling into a slicker. He just wasn't used to explaining his moves. "We're going to need water. Rain, water, bucket," he said, picking up one. "And there's a generator in the shed. I might be able to get it going. Don't mess with my stuff," he added, and walked back into the storm.

"Not without a tetanus shot, believe me," she muttered as the door slammed behind him.

Afraid of what she might find, she eased open a cupboard. Then another, and another. As the first three were empty, she found what she assumed were the only clean dishes in the cabin in the last one.

She poured coffee into a chipped mug, and took the first wary sip. She was delighted and stunned that the man made superior coffee.

Braced by it, she took stock of the kitchen. She couldn't just stand around in this sty and do nothing. If they were going to eat, she was going to have to figure out how to cook under these conditions.

There were plenty of cans in the pantry, among them two cans of condensed tomato soup. It was something. Cheered, she cracked open the refrigerator.

While it wasn't filthy, perhaps worse, it was very nearly empty. She frowned over three eggs, a hunk of very old cheese, a six-pack of beer—minus two— and to her delight, a bottle of excellent pinot noir.

Things were looking up.

There was a quart of milk which—after a testing sniff—proved to be fresh, and a half gallon of bottled water.

Rolling up her sleeves, Princess Camilla got to work.

Fifteen minutes later, armed with a pail of her own, she stepped outside. She could barely make out the shed through the rain. But over its drumming, she heard plenty of cursing and crashing. Deciding Del would be busy for a while yet, she switched his half-filled pail with her own, and hauled the water back inside.

If he'd had some damn light, Del thought as he kicked the little generator again, he could see to fix the stupid son of a bitch. The problem was, to get some damn light he needed to fix it.

Which meant he wasn't going to get it up and running before morning. Which meant, he thought sourly, he'd wasted the best part of an hour fumbling around in a cramped shed, and had bumped his miserable shoulder countless times.

Every inch of his body hurt in one way or the other. And he was still wet, cold and in the dark.

If it had been just himself, he wouldn't have bothered with the generator in the first place. He'd have opened a can, eaten a cold dinner and worked a bit by candlelight.

But there was the woman to think about. He hated having to think of a woman under the best of circumstances—and these were far from the best.

"Fancy piece, too," he muttered, shining the flashlight around the shed to see if there was anything he could use in the cabin. "On the run from something. Probably a rich husband who didn't buy her enough sparkles to suit her."

None of his business, he reminded himself. She'd be out of his hair the next day, and he could get back to work without interruptions.

He turned, caught his shin on the generator, jerked. And literally saw stars as he aggravated his broken collarbone. Sweat slicked over his face so that he had to slap his good hand against the wall and wait for the dizzy sickness to pass.

His injuries were the reason he wasn't still on site at the Florida dig—one that had been his baby since the beginning three seasons before. He could handle that. Someone had to do the written reports, the journals, the cataloging and lab work.

He preferred that someone be himself.

But he hated the damn inconvenience of the injuries. And the weakness that dogged him behind the pain. He could barely dress himself without jarring the broken bone, the dislocated shoulder, the bruised ribs.

He couldn't even tie his own damn shoes.

It was a hell of a situation.

Steady enough to brood over his unsteadiness, he picked up the flashlight he'd dropped and made his way back to the cabin. He stopped to pick up the pail of rainwater and swore viciously as even that weight strained his resources.

In the mudroom he set down the bucket, ditched the slicker, then headed straight for a mug in the kitchen.

When he reached for the coffeepot, he saw it wasn't there.

It took him a minute. Del didn't notice details unless he meant to notice them. Not only was the coffee missing, but so were all the dishes that had been piled in the sink, over the table and counters.

He didn't remember washing them. It wasn't a chore he bothered with until all options were exhausted. Baffled, he opened a cupboard and studied the pile of clean dishes.

The counters were clean, and the table. He snarled reflexively when he saw his notes and papers tidily stacked.

But even as he marched through the cabin, prepared to skin some of that soft, rosy skin off his unwelcome visitor, the scent of coffee—and food—hit him, and hit hard. It reminded him he hadn't eaten in hours, and buried the leading edge of his temper under appetite.

There she was, stirring a saucepot over the fire. He noted she'd jury-rigged a grill—probably one of the oven racks—bracing the ends of it with stacks of bricks.

He recalled the bricks had been piled on the front porch, but had no idea why.

Resourceful, he admitted—grudgingly—and noted that for a skinny woman, she had an excellent backside.

"I told you not to touch my stuff."

She didn't jolt. He clumped through the cabin like a herd of elephants. She'd known he was there.

"I'm hungry. I refuse to cook or to eat in a sty. The papers in the kitchen are relatively undisturbed. It's the filth I dispensed with."

And the papers, she thought, were fascinating. What she could read of his handwriting, in any case.

"I knew where everything was."

"Well." She straightened, turned to face him. "Now you'll have to find where it all is now. Which is in two ordered stacks. I have no idea how you—" She broke off as she saw the blood dripping from his hand. "Oh! What have you done?"

He glanced down, noticed the shallow slice in the back of his good hand, and sighed. "Hell. What's one more?"

But she was rushing to him, taking the wounded hand and clucking over the cut like a mother hen over a chick. "Back in the kitchen," she ordered. "You're bleeding all over the place."

It was hardly a major wound. No one had ever fussed over his cuts and scrapes—not even his mother. He supposed that was due to the fact she'd always had plenty of her own. Taken off guard, he let himself be pulled back into the kitchen where she stuck his bleeding hand into the sink.

"Stay," she ordered.

As she might have said, he mused, to a pet. Or worse—a servant.

She unearthed a rag, dumped it in the pail of water and proceeded to wash off his hand. "What did you cut it on?"

"I don't know. It was dark."

She clucked again, as she examined the cleaned cut. "Do you have a first-aid kit? Antiseptic?"

"It's just a scratch," he began, but gave up and rolled his eyes at her fulminating stare. "Back there." He gestured vaguely.

She went into the mudroom, and he heard her slamming cabinet doors—and muttering.

"Vous êtes un espece de cochon, et gauche aussi."

"If you're going to curse at me, do it in English."

"I said you're a pig of a man, and clumsy as well." She sailed back in with a first-aid kit, busied herself digging out antiseptic.

He started to tell her he knew what she'd called him, then stopped himself. Why ruin what small amount of amusement he might unearth during this ordeal? "I'm not clumsy."

"Hah. That explains why your arm's in a sling and your hand is bleeding."

"This is a work-related injury," he began, but as she turned to doctor his hand, he sneezed. That basic bodily reaction to a dousing in a rainstorm had his vision wavering. He swayed, fighting for breath as his ribs screamed, and his stomach pitched.

She looked up, saw the pain turn his eyes glassy, his cheeks sheet pale.

"What is it?" Without thinking, she slid her arms around his waist to support him as his body shuddered. "You should sit."

"Just—" Trying to steady himself, he nudged her back. His vision was still gray at the edges, and he willed it to clear. "Some bruised ribs," he managed to say when he got his breath back. At her expression of guilt and horror, he bared his teeth. "Dislocated shoulder, broken clavicle—work-related."

"Oh, you poor man." Sympathy overwhelmed everything else. "Come, I'll help you upstairs. You need dry clothes. I'm making soup, so you'll have a hot meal. You should've told me you were seriously hurt."

"I'm not..." He trailed off again. She smelled fabulous—and she was cooking. And feeling sorry for him. Why be an idiot? "It's not so bad."

"Men are so foolish about admitting they're hurt. We'll need the flashlight."

"In my back pocket."

"Ah." She managed to brace him, shift her body. He didn't mind, not really, when her nice, firm breast nestled against his good side. Or when her long, narrow fingers slid over his butt to pull the flashlight out of his jean's pocket.

He really couldn't say he minded. And it took his mind off the pain.

He let her help him upstairs where he eased down to sit on the side of his unmade bed. From there he could watch her bustling around, finding more candles to light.

"Dry clothes," she said and started going through his dresser. He opened his mouth to object, but she turned with jeans and a sweatshirt in her arms and looked at him with a bolstering smile.

"Do you need me to help you...um, change?"

He thought about it. He knew he shouldn't—it was one step too far. But he figured if a man didn't at least think of being undressed by a beautiful woman he might as well be shot in the head and end it all.

"...No, thanks. I can manage it."

"All right then. I'm going down to see to the soup. Just call if you need help."

She hurried downstairs again, to stir the soup and berate herself.

She'd called him a pig. The poor man couldn't possibly do for himself when he was hurt and in pain. It shamed her, how impatient, how unsympathetic and ungrateful she'd been. At least she could make him as comfortable as possible now, give him a hot bowl of soup.

She went over to plump the sprung cushions of the sofa—and coughed violently at the dust that plumed up. It made her scowl again. Really, she thought, the entire place needed to be turned upside down and shaken out.

He'd said he'd fired his cleaning service because they—she—had touched his things. She didn't doubt that for a minute. The man had an obviously prickly temperament. But she also imagined finances could be a problem. Being an archaeologist, he probably subsisted on grants and that sort of thing.

She'd have to find a way to send him payment for the night's lodging—after she sold her watch.

When he came back down, she had bowls and cups and folded paper towels in lieu of napkins on the scarred coffee table. There was candlelight, and the glow from the fire, and the good scent of hot soup.

She smiled—then stared for just a moment. His hair was dry now, and she could see it wasn't brown. Or not merely brown as she'd assumed. It was all shot through with lighter streaks bleached out, she imagined, from the sun. It curled a bit, a deep and streaky oak tone, over the neck of the sweatshirt.

A gorgeous head of hair, she could admit, with a rough and tumbled style that somehow suited those bottle-green eyes.

"You'll feel better when you eat."

He was already feeling marginally better after swallowing one of his pain pills. The throbbing was down to an irritating ache. He was counting on the hot food smoothing that away.

He'd have killed for a hot shower, but a man couldn't have everything.

"What's for dinner?"

"Potage." She gave it a deliberately elegant sound. *"Crème de tomate avec pomme de terre."* Laughing, she tapped her spoon against the pot. "You had plenty of cans, so I mixed the soup with canned potatoes and used some of your milk. It'd be a great deal better with some herbs, but your pantry didn't run to them. Sit down. Relax. I'll serve."

Under normal circumstances, he didn't care to be pampered. At least he didn't think so. He couldn't actually remember ever having *been* pampered. Regardless, it wasn't what anyone could call a normal evening, and he might as well enjoy it.

"You don't look like the type who'd cook—more like the type who has a cook."

That made her frown. She thought she looked like a very normal, very average woman. "I'm a very good cook." She spooned up soup. Because it had interested her, she'd taken private lessons with a cordon bleu chef. "Though this is my first attempt over an open fire."

"Looks like you managed. Smells like it, too." It was his idea of praise—as his anticipatory grunt was his idea of thanks when she handed him his bowl.

"I wasn't sure what you'd like to drink. Coffee, or the milk? There's beer...and wine."

"Coffee. I took some meds, so I'd better back off

the alcohol.'' He was already applying himself to the soup. When she simply stood in front of him, waiting, he spared her a glance. ''What?''

She bit back a sigh. Since the man didn't have the courtesy to offer, she'd have to ask. ''I'd enjoy a glass of wine, if you wouldn't mind.''

''I don't care.''

''Thank you.'' Keeping her teeth gritted, she poured his coffee, then headed to the kitchen. How, she wondered, did a man get through life with no manners whatsoever? She opened the wine, and after a brief hesitation, brought the bottle back with her.

She'd have two glasses, she decided, and send him the cost of the bottle along with the money for lodging.

Since he'd already scraped down to the bottom of the bowl, she served him a second, took one for herself, then settled down.

She had suffered through countless tedious dinner parties, official events and functions. Surely she could get through a single stormy evening with Delaney Caine.

''So, you must travel considerably in your work.''

''That's part of it.''

''You enjoy it?''

''It'd be stupid to do it otherwise, wouldn't it?''

She pasted on her diplomat's expression and sipped her wine. ''Some have little choice in certain areas of their lives. Their work, where they live. How they live. I'm afraid I know little about your field. You study…bones?''

''Sometimes.'' He shrugged slightly when she lifted an eyebrow. Chitchat, he thought. He'd never seen the point of it. ''Civilizations, architecture, habits, traditions, religions, culture. Lapping over into anthropology. And bones because they're part of what's left of those civilizations."

"What're you looking for in your studies?"

"Answers."

She nodded at that. She always wanted answers. "To what questions?"

"All of them."

She rose to pour him another mug of coffee. "You're ambitious."

"No. Curious."

When her lips curved this time it wasn't her polite smile. It was generous and warm and slid beautifully over her face, into her eyes. And made his stomach tighten. "That's much better than ambition."

"You think?"

"Absolutely. Ambition can be—usually is—narrow. Curiosity is broad and liberated and open to possibilities. What do your bones tell you?" She laughed again, then gestured to the cluttered side table before she sat again. "Those bones."

What the hell, he thought. He had to write it up anyway. It wouldn't hurt to talk it through—in a limited fashion.

"That she was about forty-five years old when she died," he began.

"She?"

"That's right. Native American female. She'd had several fractures—leg and arm, probably from that fall—several years before she died. Which indicates that her culture was less nomadic than previously thought, and that the sick and injured were tended, treated."

"Well, of course, they would tend to her."

"There's no 'of course' about it. In some cultures, injuries of that type, the type that would incapacitate and prevent the wounded from pulling her weight in the tribe, would have resulted in abandonment."

"Ah well. Cruelty is nothing new," she murmured.

"No, and neither is efficiency, or survival of the fittest. But in this case, the tribe cared for the sick and injured, and buried their dead with respect and ceremony. Probably buried within a day. She, and others unearthed in the project, were wrapped in a kind of yarn made from native plants. Complex weave," he continued, thinking aloud now rather than talking to Camilla. "Had to have a loom, had to take considerable time. Couldn't have moved nomadically. Semipermanent site. Plenty of game there—and seeds, nuts, roots, wood for fires and huts. Seafood."

"You know all this from a few bones?"

"What?"

She saw, actually saw him click back to her. The way his eyes focused again, clouded with vague annoyance. "You learned this from a few bones?" she repeated.

It was barely the surface of what he'd learned— and theorized. "We got more than a few, and findings other than bones."

"The more you learn, the more you understand how they lived, why they did things. What came from their lives, and what was lost. You look for—is this right—how they built their homes, cooked their food. How they raised their children, buried their dead. What deities they worshiped, and battles they fought. And in the end, how we evolved from that."

It was, he admitted, a nice summary for a layman.

There was a brain inside the classy package. "That's close enough."

"Perhaps the women cooked soup over an open fire."

The glint of humor caught him, had him nearly smiling back. "Women have been copping kitchen duty since the start. You've got to figure there's a reason for that."

"Oh, I do. Men are more inclined to beat their chests and pick fights than see to the more basic, and less heroic tasks."

"There you go." He rose. Despite the coffee, he was dragging. It was the main reason he skipped the pain pills as often as possible. "I'm going up. Spare bed's in the first room, left of the stairs."

Without a thank-you, a good-night or even one of his occasional grunts, he left Camilla alone in front of the fire.

Chapter Three

I don't know what to make of my host, Camilla wrote. It was late now, and she'd opted to huddle on the miserable sofa in front of the fire as the spare room upstairs had been chilly and damp—and dark.

She hadn't heard a sound out of Del, and though she'd tried both the lights and the phone, she'd gotten nothing out of them, either.

I've decided to attribute his lack of social skills to the fact that his line of work puts him more in company with the long dead than the living. And to season this with some sympathy over his injuries. But I suspect he's every bit as brusque and unpardonably rude when in full, robust health.

In any case, he's interesting—and spending time with people who will treat me as they treat anyone is part of this experiment.

As a lovely side benefit of his, apparently, hermit

lifestyle, there is no television in the cabin. Imagine that, an American home without a single television set. I saw no current newspapers or magazines, either. Though some may very well be buried in the refuse heap he lives in.

The chances of such a man recognizing me, even under these oddly intimate conditions, are slim to none. It's very reassuring.

Despite his odd choice of living arrangements when not actively working on a dig, he's obviously intelligent. When he spoke of his work—however briefly—there was a spark there. A sense of curiosity, of seeking answers, that appeals to me very much. Perhaps because I'm seeking something myself. Within myself.

Though I know it was not entirely appropriate behavior, I read through more of his papers when I was certain he was in his room upstairs. It's the most fascinating work! As I understand from the scribbles, he's part of a team which has discovered a site in south-central Florida. Deep in the black peat that was being dug for a pond in a development, the bones from an ancient people—tests show seven thousand years ancient—were unearthed.

His notes and papers are so disordered, I'm unable to follow the exact procedure, but The Bardville Research Project began from this discovery, and Delaney has worked on it for three years.

Their discoveries are amazing to me. A toddler buried with her toys, artifacts of bone, antler and wood, some of them inscribed with patterns. A strong sense of ritual and appreciation of beauty. There are sketches—I wonder if he did them himself. Quite intricate and well-done sketches.

There are so many notes and papers and pieces. Honestly, they're spread willy-nilly over the cabin. I would love to organize them all and read about the entire project from its inception through to the present. But it's impossible given the state of things, not to mention my departure in the morning.

For myself, I'm progressing. I'm sleeping better, night by night. My appetite's returned, and I've indulged it perhaps a little more than I should. Today, after a long drive, and a minor accident, I spent a considerable amount of time on elemental domestic chores. Fairly physical. Less than two weeks ago the most mundane task seemed to sap all my energy— physically, emotionally, mentally. Yet after this day, I feel strong, almost energized.

This time, this freedom to simply be, was exactly the remedy I needed.

I'm taking more, a few weeks more, before Camilla MacGee blends back into Camilla de Cordina again.

In the morning, the bright, bold sunlight slanted directly across Del's eyes. He shifted, seeking the dark and the rather amazing dream involving a lanky redhead with a sexy voice and gilded eyes. And rolled on his bad side.

He woke cursing.

When his mind cleared, he remembered the lanky redhead was real. The fact that she was real, and sleeping under the same roof, made him a little uneasy about the dream. He also remembered the reason the classy dish was in the spare bed was that her car was in a ditch, and the power and phones were out.

That meant, rather than a hot shower, he was going to take a dip in a cold pond. He gathered what he needed, and started downstairs. He stopped when he heard her singing.

The pretty voice with its faintly exotic accent seemed out of place in his cabin. But he couldn't fault the aroma of fresh coffee.

The coffee was heating on the fire, and she was in the kitchen, rooting around in the pantry.

He saw that the floor had been washed. He had no idea it had any shine left in it, but she'd managed to draw it out. There were wildflowers stuck in a tumbler on the kitchen table.

She had opened the kitchen window, the door to the mudroom and the door beyond that so the fresh and balmy air circled through.

She stepped back, a small can of mushrooms in her hand—and muffled a short scream when she saw him behind her.

He hadn't clomped this time. He was barefoot and bare-chested, clad only in a ragged pair of sweatpants and his sling.

His shoulders were broad, and his skin—apparently all of it—was tanned a dusky gold. The sweatpants hung loose over narrow hips, revealing a hard, defined abdomen. There were fascinating ropy muscles on his uninjured arm.

She felt the instinctive female approval purr through her an instant before she saw the sunburst of bruises over his right rib cage.

"My God." She wanted to touch, to soothe, and barely stopped herself. "That must be very painful."

"It's not so bad. What're you doing?"

"Planning breakfast. I've been up a couple of hours, so I'm ready for it."

"Why?"

"Because I'm hungry."

"No." He turned away to find a mug. If he didn't have caffeine immediately, he was going to disintegrate. "Why have you been up a couple of hours?"

"Habit."

She knew most people's fantasies of a princess, and the reality of the life were dramatically different. In official mode, it was rare for her to sleep beyond 6:00 a.m. Not that Delaney Caine knew she had an official mode.

"Bad habit," he muttered and strode back to the coffeepot.

She got her own mug and went back with him. "I took a walk earlier," she began. "It's a gorgeous day and a beautiful spot. The forest is lovely, simply lovely. And there's a pond. I saw deer watering, and there's foxglove and wild columbine in bloom. It answered the question for me why anyone would live here. Now I wonder how you can bear to leave it."

"It's still here whenever I get back." He drank the first mug of coffee the way a man wandering in the desert drank water. Then closing his eyes, he breathed again. "Thank you, God."

"The power's still out. We have three eggs—which we'll have scrambled with cheese and mushrooms."

"Whatever. I've got to wash up." He picked up his travel kit again, then just stopped and stared at her.

"What is it?"

Del shook his head. "You've got some looks, sister. Some looks," he repeated with a mutter and strode out.

It hadn't sounded like a compliment, she thought.

Regardless her stomach fluttered, and kept fluttering when she went back to the kitchen to mix the eggs.

He ate the eggs with a single-mindedness that made her wonder why she'd worried about flavor.

The fact was, he was in serious heaven eating something he hadn't thrown together himself. Something that actually tasted like food. Happy enough that he didn't mention he'd noticed that his papers in the living room had been shuffled into tidy piles.

She earned extra points by not chattering at him. He hated having someone yammering away before he'd gotten started on the day.

If her looks hadn't been such a distraction he might have offered her a temporary job cleaning the cabin, cooking a few meals. But when a woman looked like that—and managed to sneak into your dreams only hours after you'd laid eyes on her—she was trouble.

The sooner she was out and gone, the better all around.

As if she'd read his mind, she got to her feet and began to clear the table. She spoke for the first time since they'd sat down.

"I know I've been an inconvenience, and I appreciate your help and hospitality, but I'll need to ask another favor, I'm afraid. Could you possibly drive me to the nearest phone, or town or garage? Whichever is simpler for you."

He glanced up. Camilla, whatever the rest of her real name was, had class as well as looks. He didn't like the fact that her easy grace made him feel nasty for wanting to boot her along.

"Sure. No problem." Even as he spoke, he heard the sound of a car bumping down his lane. Rising, he went out to see who the hell else was going to bother him.

Camilla walked to the window. The instant she saw the car marked Sheriff, she backed up again. Police, she thought uneasily, were trained observers. She preferred avoiding direct contact.

Del caught her quick move out of the corner of his eye, frowned over it, then stepped outside.

"Hey there, Del." Sheriff Larry Risener was middle-aged, athletic and soft-spoken. Del had known him since he'd been a boy.

"Sheriff."

"Just doing a check. Whopping storm last night. Power and phones are out for most of the county."

"Including here. Any word when we'll have it back?"

"Well." Risener smiled, scratched his cheek. "You know."

"Yeah. I know."

"Saw a compact sedan in a ditch a few miles down the road here. Rental car. Looks like somebody had some trouble in the storm."

"That's right." Del leaned on the doorjamb of the mudroom. "I came along just after it happened. Couldn't call for a tow. Driver bunked here last night. I was about to drive down to Carl's, see what he can do about it."

"All right then. Didn't want to think some tourist was wandering around in the woods somewhere. I can radio Carl's place, give him the location. Save you a trip that way, and he can swing by and let you know what's what."

"I'd appreciate that."

"Okay then. How're you doing? The shoulder and all."

"It's better. Only hurts like a bitch about half the time now."

"Bet. You hear from your folks?"

"Not in about a week."

"You give them my regards when you do," Risener said as he strolled back to his cruiser. "My youngest still prizes those fossils your mother gave him."

"I'll do that." Del waited until the cruiser eased down the lane and out of sight. Then he simply turned, aware Camilla had stepped into the mudroom behind him. "Are you in trouble with the law?"

"No." Surprise at the question had her voice jumping, just a little. "No, of course not," she added firmly.

When he turned those green eyes were sharp, fully focused on her face. "Don't string me along."

She folded her hands, calmed herself. "I haven't broken any laws. I'm not in trouble with or wanted by any authorities. I'm simply traveling, that's all, and prefer not to explain to the police that I don't have any particular destination."

Her voice was steady now, and her gaze clear and level. If she was a liar, Del thought, she was a champ. At the moment it was easier to take her word.

"All right. It'll take Carl a good hour to get to your car and swing by here. Find something to do. I've got work."

"Delaney." She knew she should thank him for taking her word, but part of her was still insulted he'd questioned it. Still, she owed him for what he'd done—and she always paid her debts. "I imagine it's difficult for you to compile your notes and papers one-handed. I have two, and I'd be happy to lend them out for an hour.''

He didn't want her underfoot. That was number one. But the fact was, he wasn't getting a hell of a lot done on his own. And if he had his eye on her, she couldn't go around tidying up his papers behind his back. ''Can you use a keyboard?''

''Yes.''

He frowned at her hands. Soft, he thought. The kind that were accustomed to weekly manicures. He doubted they'd do him much good, but it was frustrating to try to transcribe with only five working fingers.

''All right, just…sit down or something. And don't touch anything,'' he added as he walked out of the room.

He came back with a laptop computer. ''Battery's good for a couple of hours. I've got backups, but we won't need them.'' He set it down, started to fight to open it.

''I can do it.'' She brushed him away.

''Don't do anything else,'' he ordered and walked out again. He came back struggling a bit with a box. He simply snarled when she popped up to take it from him. ''I've got it. Damn it.''

She inclined her head—regally, he thought. ''It's frustrating, I'm sure, to be physically hampered. But stop snapping at me.''

When she sat again, folding her hands coolly, he dug into the box and muttered. ''You're just going to type, that's it. I don't need any comments, questions or lectures.'' He dumped a pile of loose papers, clippings, photos and notebooks on the table, pawed through them briefly. ''Need to open the document.''

She simply sat there, hands folded, mouth firmly shut.

"I thought you could use a keyboard."

"I can. But as you've just ordered me not to ask questions, I'm unable to ask which document you might like me to open, out of which program."

He snarled again, then leaning over her and started hitting keys himself. His nose ended up nearly buried in her hair—which annoyed him. It was soft, shiny, fragrant. Female enough to have the juices churning instinctively. He beetled his eyebrows and concentrated on bringing up the document he wanted.

Without thinking, she turned her head. Her mouth all but brushed his, shocking them both into jerking back. He shot her a fulminating, frustrated glare and stuck his good hand into his pocket.

"That's the one. There."

"Oh." She had to swallow, hard, and fight the urge to clear her throat. She took quiet, calming breaths instead. His eyes were so *green,* she thought.

"You have to page down to the end." He'd nearly stepped forward again to do it himself before he remembered he'd be on top of her again. "I need to pick it up there."

She did so with a casual efficiency that satisfied him. Cautious now, he circled around her for his reading glasses, then plucked from the disordered pile the precise notes he needed.

His eyes, she thought, looked even more green, even more intense, when he wore those horn-rims.

"Interred with the remains are plant materials," he began, then scowled at her. "Are you going to sit there or hit the damn keys?"

She bit back an angry remark—she would *not* sink to his level, and started to type.

"It's probable the plants, such as the intact prickly pear pad which was retrieved, were food offerings buried with the dead. A number of seeds were found in the stomach areas of articulated skeletons."

She typed quickly, falling into the rhythm of his voice. A very nice voice, she thought, when it wasn't snarling and snapping. Almost melodious. He spoke of gourds recovered in another burial, theorizing that the plant specimen may have been grown locally from seeds brought from Central or South America.

He made her see it, she realized. That was his gift. She began to form a picture in her mind of these people who had traveled to the riverbank and made a home. Tended their children, cared for their sick and buried their dead with respect and ceremony in the rich peaty soil.

"Chestnut trees?" She stopped, turned to him, breaking his rhythm with her enthusiasm. "You can tell from pollen samples that there were chestnut trees there nine thousand years ago? But how can you—"

"Look, I'm not teaching a class here." He saw the spark in her eyes wink out, turning them cool and blank. And felt like a total jerk. "Jeez. Okay, there's a good twelve feet of peat, it took eleven thousand years since the last ice age to build up to that point."

He dug through his papers again and came up with photos and sketches. "You take samples—different depths, different samples, and you run tests. It shows the types of plants in the area. Changes in climate."

"How does it show changes in climate?"

"By the types of plants. Cold, warm, cold, warm." He tapped the sketches. "We're talking eons here, so we're talking a lot of climatic variations. Leaves, seeds, pollen fall into the pond, the peat preserves them—it creates an anaerobic atmosphere—shuts out the oxygen,'' he explained. ''No oxygen, no bacterial or fungi growth, slows decay.''

''Why would they have buried their dead in a pond?''

''Could've been a religious thing. There's swamp gas, and it'd cause the pond to glow at night. Methane bubbles up, it gives the illusion—if you're into that stuff—that the water breathes. Death stops breath.''

Poetic, she thought. ''So they might have chosen it to bring breath back to their dead. That's lovely.''

''Yeah, or it could've been because without shovels for digging, it was easier to plug a hole in the muck.''

''I like the first explanation better.'' And she smiled at him, beautifully.

''Yeah, well.'' Since her smile tended to make his throat go dry, he turned away to pour coffee. And was momentarily baffled not to see the pot.

''It's in the other room,'' she said, reading his expression perfectly. ''Would you like me to put on a fresh pot?''

''Yeah, great, fine.'' He looked down at his watch, then remembered he wasn't wearing one. ''What's the time?''

''It's just after eleven.''

Alone, he paced the kitchen, then stopped to glance over what had been transcribed. He was forced to admit it was more—a great deal more—than he'd have managed on his own with his injuries.

A couple of weeks at this pace and he could have the articles done—the most irritating of his tasks—

while still giving an adequate amount of attention to organizing lab reports and cataloging.

A couple of weeks, he thought, giving his shoulder a testing roll. The doctors had said it would take a couple more weeks for him to have his mobility back. The fact was, they'd said it would be more like four weeks before he'd be able to really pull his own weight again. But in his opinion doctors were always pessimistic.

He should hire a temp typist or something. Probably should. But jeez, he hated having some stranger in his hair. Better to invest in a voice-activated computer. He wondered how long it would take him to get one, set it up and get used to it.

"Coffee'll take a few minutes." Camilla sat back down, placed her fingers over the keys. "Where were we?"

Staring out the kitchen window, he picked up precisely where he left off. Within minutes, he'd forgotten she was there. The quiet click of the keys barely registered as he talked of cabbage palms and cattail roots.

He'd segued into fish and game when the sound of tires interrupted. Puzzled, he pulled off his glasses and frowned at the red tow truck that drove up his lane.

What the hell was Carl doing here?

"Is that the garage?"

He blinked, turned. His mind shifted back, and with it a vague irritation. "Right. Yeah."

Carl was fat as a hippo and wheezed as he levered himself out of the cab of the wrecker. He took off his cap, scratched his widening bald spot, nodded as Del came outside.

"Del."

"Carl."

"How's the folks?"

"Good, last I heard."

"Good." Carl's eyes squinted behind the lenses of amber lensed sunglasses when he spotted Camilla. "That your car down the road a piece, miss?"

"Yes. Were you able to get it out?"

"Not as yet. Took a look at it for you. Got a busted headlight. Wrecked your oil pan. Left front tire's flat as a pancake. Looks to me like you bent the wheel some, too. Gonna have to replace all that before you're back on the road."

"I see. Will you be able to fix it?"

"Yep. Send for the parts once I get it in the shop. Shouldn't take more'n a couple days."

A couple of days! She readjusted her plans to drive on by evening. "Oh. All right."

"Towing, parts, labor, gonna run you about three hundred."

Distress flickered over her face before she could stop it, though she did manage to swallow the sound of it that rose up in her throat. Three hundred was twenty more than she had left in cash.

The interlude, she realized as she gnawed over it, was going to leave her flat broke. She couldn't call the car rental company as she wasn't on their records and that left her no option but to call home for funds. The idea of it made her feel like a failure.

Her silence, and the worried look in her eyes had Carl shifting his feet. "Ah...I can do with a hundred down. You can pay the balance when the work's done."

"I'll just go get the money."

She'd work something out, Camilla promised herself as she went back inside, and upstairs for her wallet. There had to be a way she could sell the watch—or something—within the next day or two. She had enough for a motel, for food until the car was repaired. As long as she was careful.

She'd figure something out in the meantime. She was good at solving problems.

But her stomach was busy sinking as she counted out the hundred dollars. It was, she discovered, lowering to need money. An experience she'd never had before—and, she acknowledged, likely one that was good for her.

A hundred-eighty and some change left, she mused, tucked into a wallet that had cost more than twice that. Let that be a lesson to you, she ordered herself, and went back downstairs.

Del was in the kitchen again, going through more notes.

"I thought I'd ask the tow-truck operator to give me a lift into town."

"He's gone."

"Gone?" She rushed to the window, stared out. "Where?"

"To deal with your car."

"But I haven't paid him yet."

"He put it on my account. Are you going to get that coffee?"

"On your account." Embarrassed pride stiffened her spine. "No. I have the money."

"Good, you can pay me when your car's up and running. I want some damn coffee."

He grabbed a mug and strode off. She marched right after him. "Here, take this."

He ignored her and the money she held out, instead going through the process of taking the pot off the fire, carrying it to the table so he could pour it into the mug, carrying it back again, then picking up the mug.

The woman was quivering with temper, he noted. Which was pretty interesting. He gave her points for being pissed. She wasn't used to being obligated, he decided. Or being in financial straights. There was money somewhere—she was wearing a few grand in that slim, Swiss efficiency on her wrist. But, at the moment, it wasn't in her wallet.

That was a puzzle, but he wasn't going to make it his business to solve it.

He'd felt sorry for her—not a usual reaction in him—when he'd seen all that worry cross her face. And he'd admired her quick control of it. She hadn't fluttered or whined, or used her looks to soften Carl up and cut a better deal.

She'd sucked it up. That he respected.

And it had occurred to him he could give her a hand, and solve one of his own problems without making either of them feel uptight about it.

"I figure you earned about twenty this morning," he told her. "Figuring ten bucks an hour for the work. I'll give you that for the keyboarding, and you can earn off the bed and meals by cleaning this place up, doing the cooking. If Carl says a couple days, you figure four. In four days, you'll have a place to stay and pay off the repair bill."

She stared at him, let it sink in. "You want me to work for you. To...do your housekeeping?"

"Been doing it anyway, haven't you? You get a

bunk for four days, I don't lose time with my work, and we part square at the end of it.''

She turned away, in what he assumed was embarrassment. He'd have been surprised, and confused, to see she had a huge grin and was fighting off laughter.

Oh, what the media would do with it, Camilla thought as she bit back chuckles. Camilla of Cordina paying for a roof over her head by scrubbing floors, heating up cans of soup and typing up notes on bones and elderberry seeds.

''How the princess spent her summer vacation.'' She could see the headline now.

She had to squeeze her eyes shut and bite her lip to keep the laughter from tumbling out.

She should refuse, of course. Give him the hundred dollars, beg a ride to town where she could contact her parents for a small loan or pawn the watch.

But, Lord, it was so *delicious*. And so wonderfully out of character. Wasn't that precisely the purpose of this quest?

No televisions, no newspapers with her image on them. Interesting work in a beautiful part of the country she'd never spent time in. Learning things she found far more compelling than anything she'd studied in school and knowing she was making a positive impact solely on her own skills. Not because of who she was, or any obligations or favors—but most importantly because it was her choice.

No, she couldn't possibly walk away from the opportunity that had just fallen into her lap.

''I'm very grateful.'' Her voice trembled a bit with suppressed humor—which he mistook for the onset of tears.

Nothing could have frightened him more.

"It's a fair deal, that's all. Don't get all sloppy about it."

"A very fair deal." She turned back, eyes shining, and struggled to keep her tone casual and brisk. "Accepted," she added, and held out a hand.

He ignored the hand because he'd added a personal stipulation to the deal. He would not, in any way, shape or form, touch her.

"I'm going to get the generator started, in case we don't get the power back. Clean something up. Just don't touch my stuff."

Camilla waited until she heard the rear doors slam behind him before she sat down and let the gales of laughter roll.

Chapter Four

An hour later, thoroughly appalled with the state of the cabin now that she had given it a thorough assessment, Camilla sailed into the shed. She was armed with a long list.

"You need supplies."

"Hand me that damn wrench."

She picked up the tool and considered herself beyond civilized for not simply bashing him over the head with it. "Your home is an abomination. I'll require cleaning supplies—preferably industrial strength. And if you want a decent meal, I'll need some food to stock the kitchen. You have to go into town."

He battled the bolt into submission, shoved the switch on. And got nothing but a wheezy chuckle out of the generator. "I don't have time to go into town."

"If you want food for your belly and clean sheets on which to sleep, you'll make time."

He used the wrench to beat viciously at the generator, then gave it three solid kicks. Much too accustomed to the male response to irritating inanimate objects to be surprised, Camilla simply stood where she was, list in hand.

When he'd finished cursing, she angled her head. "I've always wondered why men refer to uncooperative machines with crude female euphemisms."

"Because they fit like a glove." He leaned over, slapped on the switch and grunted with satisfaction as the generator let out a loud belch and began to run.

"Now that you've accomplished that amazing feat, you'll want to clean up before you go fill this list."

Eyes narrowed on her face, he picked up the wrench again, weighed it consideringly in his hand.

The implication wasn't lost on her. She simply stuck out her chin.

He tossed the wrench aside, snatched the list and smeared it with the motor oil on his fingers. "I hate bossy women."

"I can't stand crude men. We'll both just have to live with it, since I'm currently washing your underwear."

The faintest glint of humor flicked into his eyes. "You've got plenty of starch. Just don't use any on my shorts."

They started for the door at the same time, and ended up jammed together. Her hand went automatically to his chest where she felt the surprised kick of his heart match hers.

"You're going to have to keep out of my way," he told her.

"You'll have to watch where you're going, then."

She saw, with reluctant excitement, his gaze lower, and linger on her mouth. In response, her lips parted on one quiet and catchy breath.

"You got that right, sister," he muttered, and squeezed out of the door.

"Well." She breathed out, rubbing her finger experimentally over lips that felt just a little too warm. "Well, well."

She was angry, exhausted and energized—in a way she hadn't been in a very long time. Alive, whole, healthy and, she realized, interested. It was something to think about.

Del discovered, very quickly, he didn't care to be an errand boy. Shopping cut deeply into his day, and half the items on her list had him scratching his head in frustration.

What the hell was chervil, and why did it have to be fresh?

What the devil did she need with *two* dozen eggs?

And three gallons of bleach.

Maybe she was going to poison him with it, he mused as he drove back to the cabin. She'd looked mad enough to, behind that cool, queen-to-peasant stare she tended to aim at him.

That was some face she had, he reflected. The kind that kicked a man right in the gut. Then you added on the voice, those legs that seemed to go straight up to her ears, and you had one dangerous female.

He was starting to regret that he'd felt sorry for her.

Still, he knew how to be careful around dangerous packages. And she was, after all, no more than a handy tool for the next few days. So he'd give her a wide berth when they weren't actively working, keep his hands to himself at all times and do his best to think of her as a nonsexual entity.

Then when he pulled up behind the cabin and she came running out, his heart all but stopped. Nonsexual? A tool? The woman was a weapon—and a lethal one at that, he decided.

She was laughing, her face flushed with it as she pulled open the door and began to haul out grocery bags. ''The power came back on. I never thought I'd be so delighted with something as basic as a working light switch. Still no phone service, but I'm sure that's next.''

He snagged a bag and followed her inside. She walked across the dirt and gravel, he thought, as if she were gliding across the polished marble floor of a ballroom. He decided it had something to do with all that leg. Which he wasn't, of course, paying any attention to. Whatsoever.

''How many people are you planning to feed for the next few days?''

''Oh, don't be cranky.'' She waved him off and began to unload supplies. ''I'll make you a sandwich as soon as these are put away.''

She knew how to make a sandwich, he had to give her that. He ate, and ate well, in his now spotless kitchen, his mood improving as he scanned the next batch of notes. His ribs ached a bit, but the discomfort had eased to tolerable with just aspirin.

When he was done, he dictated for another three hours while she transcribed. She interrupted now and then, but her questions didn't bother him as much.

The fact was, they were good questions, the kind that made him think. He did classroom duty from time to time, though it was never his first choice. He was forced to admit that the majority of students professing a desire to make a career in the field didn't have as quick an understanding of the *point* as she did.

He caught himself studying the long line of her neck. The graceful curve and arch of it. Mortified, he turned away, pushed himself back into his notes and forgot her.

She knew he'd been staring, just as she knew he'd switched her off again as easily as a finger flicked a light from on to off.

She found she liked it—all the aspects. His interest, his annoyance with it and the focus that allowed him to dismiss it.

His interest had nothing to do with her family, her blood or her rank. It was the first time in her life she'd been utterly sure of that, and the response inside her was quick and pleased. As to the annoyance she could sense him feeling, that was purely satisfying.

He saw her as a woman, first and last. Not an image, not a title. And that made her feel like a woman. He was attracted to her and didn't want to be. That gave her a lovely edge of control—an essential female control that wasn't weighed down with royal command.

And his focus, well, that attracted *her*. It was a kind of skill she respected, and stemmed from willpower, intellect and passion for his work.

It also challenged her. Though she knew it would be wise to resist that challenge. She was, after all, essentially alone with him—a man she knew little about—and flirting with that focus, trying to undermine it for her own curiosity and satisfaction might have…consequences.

Then again, what was a quest without consequences?

When he paused long enough, she rolled her stiff shoulders, smiled over at him. "Would you mind if we took a break?"

She watched him come back to the present, back to the room, back to her. Felt his gaze, sexy and scholarly behind his reading glasses, slide over her as she rose to stretch.

"I'm not finished," he told her.

"We can pick it up again after dinner, if you like." She kept her smile easy. "I could use a walk before I start cooking. Do you ever walk in the woods, Del?"

There was the faintest hum of invitation in her voice. He was sure—damn sure—it was deliberate. It packed a hell of a punch. He hated to think what she could do if she took a good, solid shot at a man.

"Go ahead, I've got stuff to do." He picked up more notes, dismissing her. He waited until she'd passed into the mudroom before he called out, "Watch out for snakes."

The hesitation in her stride, the faintest gasp, gave him a great deal of satisfaction.

He woke in the middle of the night with his ribs aching and his mind blurry.

He'd been dreaming of her again, damn it. This time they'd been in the kitchen working on his notes. She'd sat at the keyboard, stupendously naked.

The fantasy was juvenile enough to embarrass him.

The problem with women was they could get to you just by breathing.

He lay there a moment, willing his ribs to settle and his blood to cool.

He'd gotten through the day and the evening, hadn't he, holding on to his stipulation. He'd never touched her, not once. It would've been easy to. A finger trailed down that pretty nape while she'd typed. A brush of his hand when she'd passed him the salt over dinner.

Easy, as easy as grabbing her one-handed, diving in and finding out what that long, mobile mouth tasted like.

But he hadn't. Points for him.

Still, it made him a little nervous that he kept *thinking* about doing it.

And she was flirting with him. He'd ignored, evaded or moved in on flirtations often enough to recognize one. Especially when the woman wasn't being particularly subtle.

He'd had students—or the occasional groupie who hung around digs—put moves on him. Mostly, in his estimation, because they'd dreamed up some romantic image about the field. He put the blame squarely on Indiana Jones for that. Though those movies had been so damned entertaining he couldn't be sore about it.

He dismissed the flirtations, or fell in with them, depending on the timing, the woman and his mood. But as far as serious relationships went, he'd managed to avoid that boggy complication. The redhead had complication written all over her, so fun and games were out of the question.

He should get her a room in town. Pay for it. Move her out.

Then he thought of the pile of neatly typed pages, and the intensity of his annoyance went way down. She was a miracle worker. Not only did her help mean he didn't need to fight his way through the material on his own, but her questions, her interest and her organizational ability was actually getting him to deliver the best material he'd ever done. Not that he was going to mention that.

He thought of the meal she'd put on the table. He hadn't a clue what she'd done to that humble chicken, but she'd turned it into a feast.

He began to revise his notion that she had a rich, irritated husband or lover stashed somewhere. She was too efficient, too clever in the kitchen to be somebody's spoiled and pampered tootsie.

Which was a good thing as fantasizing about another man's woman was too close to fooling around with another man's woman. And that was on his short list of unbreakable rules.

If he moved her out, he'd be back to square one. If he moved her out, he'd be admitting he couldn't keep his hands off her. If he admitted that, well, where was he?

Giving up, he rose—remembered at the last minute to tug on sweats—and went down the hall to the bathroom. He didn't notice the sparkling tiles and neatly hung fresh towels any more than he'd have noticed soap scum and damp heaps. But the scent caught him, because it was hers.

And it tightened every muscle in his body.

He yanked his pain medication from the cabinet, then shoved it back again. Damn pills made him stupid. He'd rather toss back a handful of over-the-counter stuff and a short, neat whiskey.

He didn't allow himself to so much as glance at her bedroom door, to think—even for an instant—of her lying in bed behind it. A minute later, he realized that fantasy would've been wasted because she wasn't in bed.

He heard her voice, the quiet murmur of it coming from the kitchen. Eyes narrowed, he paused, listened. He couldn't quite make out the words, but the tone was soft, full of affection. It set his teeth on edge.

Who the hell was she talking to? He moved forward and caught the end of her conversation.

"Je t'aime aussi. Bonne nuit."

The quiet click of the phone on the receiver came an instant before he hit the lights.

She stumbled back, bit off a scream and slapped both hands to her mouth. *"Mon Dieu! Vous m'avez fait peur!"* She let out a shaky breath, shook the French out of her head. "You frightened me."

"What are you doing down here in the dark?"

She'd crept down to check the phone, and finding it working, had called home to reassure her family. She kept the lights off and her voice low to avoid exactly what was happening now. Explanations.

"The phone's back on."

"Yeah. Answer the question."

Her shoulders went back, her chin went up. "I didn't realize I was meant to stay in my room like a child after bedtime," she tossed back. "I'm repaying you for the lodging, and assumed I was free to make use of the house."

"I don't give a damn if you dance a tango in the moonlight. I want to know why you're sneaking around and whispering on the phone in the dark."

She gave him the truth, and coated it with ice. "I

couldn't sleep. I came down for a drink and checked the phone. When I discovered it was in order, I made a call. Don't worry, I reversed the charges. If my mobile worked in this...backwater, I wouldn't have presumed to use yours. And having the courtesy to be quiet when another person in the house was, *presumably,* sleeping isn't sneaking.''

It was reasonable. It rang true. So he nodded, slowly. "Fine. You want to check in with your husband or boyfriend, go ahead. But don't prowl around like a thief.''

Her color bloomed, her eyes went burning gold. "I was not prowling, and I don't have a husband. If you must know, I spoke with my mother to reassure her I was well. Is this inquisition over?''

He hated feeling stupid so he said nothing and stepped to the cabinet for aspirin.

"I should've known.'' With an impatient huff, she took down a glass to fill it with water. "You're only more impossible when you're in pain. Here.''

"I don't want water.'' He moved around her to root at the bottle of whiskey from the pantry.

"Have the water first, you'll spoil the taste of the whiskey otherwise.'' She got down another glass, took the bottle from him and poured a tidy three fingers. "I imagine it should help the discomfort. Is it your shoulder or your ribs?''

"Ribs mostly.''

"I suppose they hurt more as they heal. Why don't you sit and I'll make you an ice pack for them.''

"I don't need a nurse.''

"Stop being such a hardhead.'' She filled a small plastic bag with ice, then wrapped it in a thin dishcloth. "Sit, drink your whiskey. Tell me about one of your other digs. Something foreign and exotic."

It amused her, pleased her, to hear her mother in her voice, the brisk indulgence of it, the tone she'd used to soothe and distract her children during illness.

"Go away." The order didn't have much punch behind it, and he sat down.

"When I was cleaning I noticed some correspondence to Dr. Caine. I was impressed." She sat, holding the cloth to her cheek and waiting for it to cool. "Where did you study?"

She was wearing a robe, the color of copper. He figured it had to be silk, and from the way it clung, shifted, that she had little to nothing on under it. In defense he closed his eyes and let the whiskey slide down his throat.

"Oxford."

"Now I'm more impressed. Delaney Caine, a doctorate degree from Oxford. How did you know you were an archaeologist?"

It was an odd way to phrase it, he thought. Not how did you become, or when did you decide, but how did you know. And it was exactly right. "I always wanted to know how and why and when. And who. Whenever I'd go on a dig with my parents—"

"Ah, they're archaeologists, too."

"Paleontologists. Dinosaurs." He kept his eyes closed, knowing between will and whiskey the ache would ease. "I liked the digs, but it seemed more exciting to me when they'd dig up something human. Pieces of pottery or tools or weapons. Something that said man walked there."

He hissed a bit through his teeth when the cooled cloth made contact with his ribs.

Poor thing, she thought sympathetically. So angry at the pain. "My brothers went through a fascination with dinosaurs. I think all boys do." She saw the strain go out of his face as the ice numbed the ache. "Were they disappointed, your parents, that you didn't go into their field?"

"Why would they be?" He let himself relax, inch by inch. An owl hooted, long, slow calls from the woods beyond the cabin. Her scent drifted over him like a gentle stroke of hands.

"Oh, tradition, I suppose. It's comforting, isn't it, to have parents who understand—at least try to understand—when you have to test yourself, try your own direction? Some of us wait too long to do so, fearing disapproval or failure."

He was relaxed, she thought, drifting toward sleep. Odd, he looked no less formidable now than he did when he was alert. Maybe it was the bones of his face, or that prickly shadow of beard. Whatever it was, it had a snake of arousal twining through her to look at him, really look at him when he was unaware.

Then his eyes opened, and that interesting face was very close to hers. She nearly eased back with instinctive courtesy, but there was a wariness in those deep green depths. An intriguing awareness that nudged her to test her power.

She stayed close, very close, and lifted a hand to give the rough stubble on his face a testing, and flirtatious, rub. "You need a shave, Dr. Caine."

He could smell her, all fresh and dewy despite the lateness of the hour. Her breath fanned lightly over his skin. And made his mouth water. "Cut it out."

"It'd be tricky to shave one-handed." She trailed

a fingertip along his jaw. Down his throat. "I could do it for you in the morning."

"I don't want a shave, and I don't like you touching me."

"Oh, you like me touching you." Surely this lust that was curling around in her belly wasn't all one-sided. "You're just afraid of it. And annoyed that I'm not afraid of you."

He grabbed her wrist with his good hand, and his fingers tightened warningly. "If you're not afraid, you're stupid." Deliberately he raked his gaze over her, an insulting pass down her body and back up again. "We're alone out here, and you've got no place to hide. I may have only one good arm, but if I decided to help myself, you couldn't stop me."

Anger danced up her spine, but there was no fear in it. No one had ever laid hands on her unless she'd allowed it. She didn't intend for that to change. "You're wrong about that. I don't hide, I confront. I'm not weak or helpless."

He tightened his grip on her wrist, fully aware his fingers would likely leave marks. He hoped they did, and she remembered it. For both their sakes. "You're a woman, and I outweigh you by close to a hundred pounds. A lot of men would use that advantage to take a sample of you. Whether you were to their taste or not. I'm more particular, and, sister, you don't appeal to me."

"Really?" Her anger was full-blown now, a state she worked to avoid. When she was angry, overcome with anger, she knew she could be incredibly rash. She did her best to cool down, to take the reins of her temper in hand. "That's fortunate for both of us then."

She eased back, tugged her arm free when his grip

on her loosened. She saw something flicker in his eyes—relief or disdain, she wasn't sure. But either way, it fanned the flames again.

"But it's a lie."

She was angry, rash—and, she supposed, incredibly stupid. But the reins of temper slipped, and she fisted both hands in his hair and crushed her mouth to his.

Her first reaction was satisfaction, pure and simple, when she heard his quick, indrawn breath. She went with it, using her lips and tongue to get a good taste of him.

And as that taste filled her, pumped inside her with an unexpected wave of heat, it led to her second reaction.

A slow and slippery meltdown.

She hadn't been prepared for it, not for need to burn through anger, every layer of it, and pull the hair trigger of her own passion. She made a little sound, both surprise and pleasure, and slid into him.

His mouth was hard, his face rough and his hair as thick and soft as mink pelt. She could feel the jackhammer of his heart, and the grip of his hand—this time vised on her nape. His teeth, then his tongue met hers. All she could think was: Give me more.

His reflexes were sluggish. It was the only excuse he could give for not shoving her away before she slid into him. And he was only human. That was the only reason he could find for his hand lifting—not to push her off, but to clamp over her neck, to keep her just where she was.

All over him.

The soft, greedy sounds she made had his blood surging, drove him to fight to deepen the kiss even as it reached depths he wasn't sure he could stand.

He wanted to swallow her whole—one wild, voracious bite. He wanted it, wanted her, more than he wanted his next breath.

He shifted, struggling to wrap his other arm around her, drag her onto his lap. The sudden careless move had bright, blinding pain smothering passion.

She jerked back. She'd felt his body go rigid, heard him fight to catch his breath, knew she'd hurt him. Concern, apologies nearly fell off her tongue before his vicious glare stopped them.

"Stay the hell away from me." He couldn't pull in any air, and his head swam. He cursed because he knew it had every bit as much to do with his body's reaction to her as it did to the pain.

"Let me help—"

"I said stay the hell away." His chair crashed to the floor as he pushed himself upright. When his vision blurred he nearly swayed, and the weakness only added to his fury. "You want a quick roll, go somewhere else. I'm not in the market."

He strode out of the house, the two doors slamming like bullets at his back.

She was thoroughly ashamed of herself, and had barely slept all night for cringing every time she replayed the scene in her head.

She'd pushed herself on him. All but *forced* herself on him. It meant nothing that she'd been angry and insulted and aroused all at once. Why if a man had behaved as she had, Camilla would have been first in line to condemn him as a brute and a barbarian.

She'd made him kiss her, taking advantage of the situation and her physical advantage. That was unconscionable.

She would have to apologize, and accept whatever payment he wanted for the offense. If that meant booting her out of the house on her ear, he had a perfect right to do so.

She hoped it wouldn't come to that.

It might have been an embarrassingly female cliché, but she stationed herself in the kitchen, only an hour after dawn, and prepared to fix him a lovely breakfast to soften him up.

Of course, she might have to adjust that to lunch, as he hadn't come back into the house until after three in the morning. When she heard him come in, she hadn't started breathing again for ten minutes, half expecting him to burst into her room, haul her out of bed and pitch her out of the window then and there.

Not that he hadn't responded to her advance, she reminded herself as shame continued to prick. He'd all but devoured her like a man starving. And if he hadn't tried to drag her closer and caused himself pain...

Well, she supposed it was best not to think of that.

She had coffee brewed, juice chilling. She'd made batter and filling for apple-cinnamon crêpes from scratch and had a generous slice of country ham waiting. Now if the bear would only lumber out of his cave.

Minutes later she heard the creak overhead that told her he was up and about. She had to wipe suddenly damp palms on her slacks before she turned to heat the griddle for his breakfast.

Because Del was also replaying the scene in his head, he was in the foulest of moods as he showered. Part of him was furious with the woman for putting him in such an impossible position. The other stood back in amazed disgust at his reaction.

He'd had a beautiful woman come on to him in a staggeringly open and avid way. A gorgeous, sexy, unattached woman had grabbed him in the middle of the night and kissed his brains out.

And he'd stormed out of the house in a huff.

What was he, crazy?

Careful, he corrected, annoyed with the internal debate. He had no problem with casual, healthy sex between consenting adults. But if there was a casual bone in Camilla's body, he'd dance a jig naked in the middle of the road to town.

The woman breathed complications.

Besides the fact, he reminded himself as he dressed, he didn't have time for fun and games. He had work to do. And when he did have time, *he* made the damn moves.

Not that it hadn't been…interesting to have that step taken out of his hands, momentarily.

The woman had a mouth like a goddess, he thought. Hot, persuasive and potent.

Better not to think about it. Much better to decide what the hell to do about it. As far as he could see, there were two choices. He could pretend it never happened, or he could fire her, drive her into town and dump her.

The latter, it seemed to him, was the safest bet all around.

He was halfway down the stairs when he smelled coffee. The siren's scent of it weakened his resolve. He could count on the fingers of one hand the number of times in his adult life he'd woken to the aroma of fresh coffee.

Then he caught the scent of grilling meat.

Plays dirty, he noted. Just like a female.

The minute he stepped into the kitchen, she turned, coffee mug in hand. Rather than hand it to him, she set it on the table. She didn't smile, but her eyes met his and stayed level.

"I want to apologize for my behavior."

The tone, judge-sober, threw him off stride. He figured the best move was to keep his mouth shut—and drink the coffee.

"It was," she continued, "completely indefensible. I took advantage of the situation and abused your hospitality. I couldn't be more sorry for it. You'd be perfectly justified in throwing me out. I hope you won't, but I won't argue if that's what you've decided to do."

Did he think she played dirty? he mused, eyeing her over the rim of his cup as she stood, solemn and patient with ham sizzling at her back. A heavyweight champ wouldn't last a full round with her.

"Let's just forget it."

Relief trickled through her, but she couldn't relax until she'd finished. "That's very generous of you." She shifted to pick up the kitchen fork and turn the meat. "I'd like to tell you I've never done anything like that before."

He thought of the kiss, the smoldering punch of it. "Like what before?"

"Pushed myself on a man." The memory of it had hot color washing into her cheeks, but she continued to cook with a steady hand. "It occurred to me afterward that if the situation had been reversed—if you had pushed yourself on me, particularly when I was incapacitated—"

"I'm not incapacitated." Irritated, he swallowed coffee, then went for more.

"Well...in any case, it occurred to me that it would've been contemptible, perhaps even criminal, so—"

"We locked lips. Beginning and end," he snapped out, growing more and more uncomfortable. "It's not a big damn deal."

She slid her gaze toward him, then away again. The deal, big or otherwise, had kept him out of his own house most of the night. So she *would* finish groveling. "A sexual act of any kind must be mutual or it's harassment. Worst, molestation."

"The day some skinny-assed woman can molest me is the day pigs go into orbit."

"I'm not skinny, assed or otherwise, but to finish. I was angry and I'm attracted to you—God knows why—and both those reactions, as well as the simple curiosity I felt, are my responsibility to control. I appreciate your acceptance of my apology. Now if you'd like to sit down, I'm going to make crêpes."

She stabbed the ham, dumped it on a plate. Before she could turn to the crêpe batter, he spun her around, clamped his hand over her throat. And lifting her to her toes closed his mouth over hers.

The fork she still held clattered to the counter. Her arms fell helplessly to her sides. It was an assault, a glorious one that made her weak-kneed, light-headed and hot-blooded all at once. Even as she started to sway toward him, he gave her a light shove. Stepped back.

"There, that clears the slate," he said, then picking up his coffee again, sat. "What kind of crêpes?"

Chapter Five

The beard irritated him. So did the woman. His ribs were a constant dull ache. As was his libido.

Work helped such nagging and unwelcome distractions. He'd always been able to lose himself in work—in fact he figured anyone who couldn't just wasn't in the right field.

He had to admit she didn't annoy him when she was helping transcribe and organize his notes. The fact was, she was such an enormous help he wondered how the devil he would get anything done when she was gone.

He considered playing on her gratitude and wheedling another couple of weeks out of her.

Then he'd be distracted by something as ridiculous as the way the light hit her hair as she sat at the keyboard. Or the way her eyes took on a glint when she looked over at him with a question or comment.

Then he'd start thinking about her. Who she was, where she was from. Why the hell she was sitting in his kitchen in the first place. She spoke French like a native, cooked like a gift from God. And over it all was a glossy sheen of class.

He hated asking people questions about themselves. Because they invariably answered them, at length. But he had a lot of questions about Camilla.

He began to calculate how he could get some information without seeming to ask the questions.

She was smart, too, he thought as she painstakingly filed and labeled on-site photographs while he pretended to study more notes. Not just educated, but there was plenty of that. If he had to guess, he'd say private schools all the way—and with that whiff of France in her voice, he'd put money on some kind of Swiss finishing school.

In any case, wherever she'd been educated, she was smart enough to let the whole matter of that little sexual snap drop.

She'd simply nodded when he'd said they were even, and had made her fancy breakfast crêpes.

He admired that, the way she'd accepted the tit for tat and had gone back to business as usual.

There was money—or there had been money. Pricey Swiss watch, silk robe. And it had been silk. He could still feel the way it had floated and slithered over his bare skin when she'd wrapped herself around him.

Damn it.

Still, she was no stranger to work. She actually seemed to *like* cooking. It was almost beyond his comprehension. Plus she'd sit at the keyboard for hours without complaint. Her typing was neat and quick, her posture perfect. And her hands as elegant as a queen's.

Breeding, he thought. The woman had breeding. The kind that gave you spine as well as a sense of fair play.

And she had the most incredible mouth.

So how did it all add up?

He caught himself scratching at the beard again, and was struck with inspiration.

"Could use a shave."

He said it casually, waited for her to glance his way. "I'm sorry?"

"A shave," he repeated. "I could use one."

Because she considered it a friendly overture, she smiled. "Can you manage it, or do you want help?"

He frowned a little, to show he was reluctant. "You ever shave a man?"

"No." She pursed her lips, angled her head. "But I've seen my father and my brothers shave. How hard can it be?"

"Brothers?"

"Yes, two." Thoughtful, she stepped to him, bending a bit to study the terrain of his face. A lot of angles, she mused. Dips and planes. There certainly wasn't anything smooth or simple about it, but that only made it challenging. "I don't see why I couldn't do it."

"It's my flesh and blood on the line, sister." Still he lifted a hand, rubbed irritably. "Let's do it."

She took the job seriously. After some debate, she decided the best spot for the event was the front porch. They'd get a little fresh air, and she'd be able to maneuver a full three hundred and sixty degrees around his chair as she couldn't in the tiny upstairs bathroom.

She dragged out a small table, and set up her tools. The wide, shallow bowl filled with hot water. The can of shaving cream, the towels, the razor.

Part of her wished it was a straight rather than a safety razor. It would've been fun to strop it sharp.

When he sat, she tied a towel around his neck. "I could trim your hair while I'm at it."

"Leave the hair alone."

She couldn't blame him. It was a marvelous head of hair, wonderfully streaky and tumbled. In any case her one attempt at cutting hair—her own—had proved she had no hidden talent for it.

"All right, just relax." She covered his face with a warm, damp towel. "I've seen this in movies. I believe it softens the beard."

When he gave a muffled grunt and relaxed, she looked out at the woods. They were so green, so thick, dappled with light and shadows. She could hear birdsong, and caught the quick flash of a cardinal—a red bullet into a green target.

No one was huddled in those shadows waiting for her to make some move that would earn them a fee for a new photograph. There were no stoic guards standing by to protect her.

The peace of it was like a balm.

"It's beautiful out today." Absently she laid a hand on his shoulder. She wanted to share this lovely feeling of freedom with someone. "All blue and green with summer. Hot, but not oppressive. In Virginia, we'd be drenched in humidity by now."

Aha! He knew he'd tagged a touch of the South in her voice. "What's in Virginia?"

"Oh, my family." Some of them, she thought. "Our farm."

As she took the towel away, his eyes—sharp and full of doubt—met hers. "You're telling me you're a farmer's daughter? Give me a break."

"We have a farm." Vaguely irritated, she picked up the shaving cream. Two farms, she thought. One in each of her countries. "My father grows soy beans, corn and so on. And raises both cattle and horses."

"You never hoed a row with those hands, kid."

She lifted a brow as she smoothed on the shaving cream. "There's been a marvelous new invention called a tractor. And yes, I can drive one," she added with some asperity.

"Hard to picture you out on the back forty."

"I don't spend much time with the crops, but I know a turnip from a potato." Brows knitted, she lifted his chin and took the first careful swipe with the razor. "My parents expected their children to be productive and useful, to make a contribution to the world. My sister works with underprivileged children."

"You said you had brothers."

"One sister, two brothers. We are four." She rinsed the razor in the bowl, meticulously scraped off more cream and stubble.

"What do you do, back on the farm?"

"A great many things," she muttered, calculating the angle from jaw to throat.

"Is that what you're running away from? Hey!"

As the nick welled blood, she dabbed at it. "It's just a scratch—which I wouldn't have made if you'd just stop talking. You say nothing for hours at a time, and now you don't shut up."

Amused, and intrigued that he'd apparently hit a nerve—he shrugged his shoulder. "Maybe I'm nervous. I've never had a woman come at me with a sharp implement."

"That is surprising, considering your personality."

"Tagging you as Rebecca of Sunnybrook Farm's surprising, considering yours. If you grew up in Virginia, where's the French pastry part come from?"

Her brows lifted above eyes lit with humor. "French pastry, is it? My mother," she said, ignoring the little twist of guilt that came from not being completely honest. Because of it, she gave him more truth—if not specifics. "We spend part of our time in Europe—and have a small farm there as well. Do this." She drew her top lip over her teeth.

He couldn't stop the grin. "Show me how to do that again?"

"Now he's full of jokes." But she laughed, then stepped between his legs, bent down and slowly shaved the area between his nose and mouth.

He wanted to touch her, to run his hand over some part of her. Any part of her. He wanted, he realized, to kiss her again. Whoever the hell she was.

Her thumb brushed his mouth, held his lip in place, then slid away. But her gaze lingered there before it tracked up to his.

And she saw desire, the dangerous burn of it in his eyes. Felt it stab inside her like the fired edge of a blade.

"Why is this, do you think?" she murmured.

He didn't pretend to misunderstand. He didn't believe in pretense. "I haven't got a clue—other than you being a tasty treat for the eyes."

She nearly smiled at that, and turned to rinse the

razor again. "Even attraction should have more. I'm not sure we even like each other very much."

"I don't have anything against you, particularly."

"Why, Delaney, you're so smooth." She laughed because it eased some of the tension inside her. "A woman hasn't a prayer against such poetry, such charm."

"You want poetry, read a book."

"I think I do like you." She considered as she came back to finish the shave. "On some odd level, I enjoy your irascibility."

"Old men are irascible. I'm young yet, so I'm just rude."

"Precisely. But you also have an interesting mind, and I find it attractive. I'm intrigued by your work." She turned his face to the side, eased in close again. "And your passion for it. I came looking for passion—not the sexual sort, but for some emotional—some intellectual passion. How strange that I should find it here, and in old bones and broken pots."

"My field takes more than passion and intellect."

"Yes. Hard work, sacrifice, sweat, perhaps some blood." She angled her head. "If you think I'm a stranger to such things, you're wrong."

"You're not a slacker."

She smiled again. "There now, you've flattered me. My heart pounds."

"And you've got a smart mouth, sister. Maybe, on some odd level, I enjoy your sarcasm."

"That's handy. Why don't you ever use my name?" She stepped back to pick up a fresh towel and wipe the smears of shaving cream left on his face. "It is my name," she said quietly. "Camilla. My mother enjoys flowers, and there were camellias on my father's farm when he took her there for the first time.''

''So, you only lied about the last name.''

''Yes.'' Testingly she ran her fingers over his cheeks. ''I think I did a fine job, and you have a nice, if complicated face. Better, by far, without the scraggly beard.''

She walked to the table, wiped her hands. ''I only want a few weeks for myself,'' she murmured. ''A few weeks to *be* myself without restrictions, responsibilities, demands, expectations. Haven't you ever just needed to breathe?''

''Yeah.'' And something in her tone, something in her eyes—both haunted—told him that, at least, was perfect truth. ''Well, there's plenty of air around here.'' He touched his face, rubbed a hand over his freshly shaved chin. ''Your car'll be ready in a couple days. Probably. You can take off then, or you can stay a week or two, and we'll keep things the way they are.''

Tears stung her eyes, though she had no idea why. ''Maybe a few days longer. Thank you. I'd like to know more about your project. I'd like to know more about you.''

''Let's just keep things the way they are. Until they change. Nice shave... Camilla.''

She smiled to herself as the screen door slammed behind him.

To demonstrate her gratitude, Camilla did her best not to annoy him. For an entire day and a half. She had the cabin scrubbed to a gleam, his photographs and sketches labeled and filed. The neatly typed pages from his notes and dictation now comprised two thick stacks.

It was time, she decided, for a change in routine.

"You need fresh supplies," she told him.

"I just bought supplies."

"Days ago, and the key word is fresh. You're out of fruit, low on vegetables. And I want lemons. I'll make lemonade. You drink entirely too much coffee."

"Without coffee: coma."

"And you're nearly out of that as well, so unless you'd like to be comatose, we have to go into town for supplies."

For the first time, he spared her a look, taking off his reading glasses to frown at her. "We?"

"Yes. I can check on the status of my car as your Carl only makes mumbling noises over the phone when I call to ask about it." She was already checking the contents of her purse, taking out her sunglasses. "So. We'll go to town."

"I want to finish this section."

"We can finish when we get back. I'm happy to drive if your shoulder's troubling you too much."

In point of fact, his shoulder barely troubled him at all now. He'd put the hours he spent restless and awake in his room at night to good use by carefully exercising it. His ribs were still miserable, but he was about ready to ditch the sling.

"Sure, I'll just let you behind the wheel of my truck since you've proven what a good driver you are."

"I'm a perfectly good driver. If the deer hadn't—"

"Yeah, yeah, well you can forget driving my truck, kid." Since he knew her well enough now to be sure she'd nag and push for the next hour, he decided to save time and aggravation and just go. "I'll drive—but you do the grocery thing."

When he simply stood, frowning, she angled her head. "If you're trying to remember where you put your keys, they're in the ignition of your precious truck, where you left them."

"I knew that," he muttered and started out. "Are we going or not?"

As pleased as if she'd been offered a night on the town, she hurried after him. "Is there a department store? I could use some—"

"Hold it." He stopped short at the back door so that she bumped solidly into him. "No, there's not, and don't get the idea we're going on some spree. You want lemons, we'll get some damn lemons, but you're not dragging me off on some girl safari looking for shoes and earrings and God knows."

She had a small—and perfectly harmless—weakness for earrings. Her mouth moved into something perilously close to a pout. "I merely want some eye cream."

He tugged her sunglasses down her nose, gave her eyes a hard look. "They're fine."

She rolled them at his back as he continued toward the truck, but she decided not to push the issue. Until they were in town. Now, it was better to distract him.

"I wonder," she began as she hitched herself into the cab of the truck, "if you could tell me how radiocarbon dating works."

"You want a workshop—"

"Yes, yes, take a course. But just a thumbnail explanation. I do better with the transcribing if I have a picture in my head."

His sigh was long-suffering as the truck bumped along the lane toward the main road. "Carbon's in the atmosphere. You got trillions of atoms of carbon to every one atom of radioactive Carbon 14. Plants absorb Carbon 14, animals absorb it by—"

"Eating the plants," she finished, pleased with herself.

He shot her a look. "And other animals. Absorbed, it starts to disintegrate. It gets replenished from the atmosphere or from food. Until whatever's absorbed, it dies. Anyway, in a plant or an animal it gives off about fifteen disintegration rays every minute, and they can be detected by a Geiger counter. The rest is just math. The dead source loses radioactivity at a rate... Why am I talking to myself?"

"What?" She dragged her attention back. "I'm sorry. It's just so beautiful. I missed so much in the storm. It's so green and gorgeous. A bit like Ireland, really, with all those hills."

She caught the glint that could only be sun flashing off water. "And a lake, all the lovely trees. It's all so still and quiet."

"That's why most people live in this part of Vermont. We don't like crowds and noise. You want those, you don't come to the NEK, you go west to Lake Champlain."

"The NEK?"

"Northeast Kingdom."

The name made her smile. So, she thought, she'd slipped away from a principality for a time, and landed in a kingdom. "Have you always lived here?"

"Off and on."

She gave a little cry of delight as they approached a covered bridge. "Oh, it's charming!"

"It gets you over the stream," Del said, but her pleasure was infectious. Sometimes he forgot to look around, to take satisfaction in the pretty piece of the world where he often made his home.

They rattled over the bridge toward the white church spires that rose over the trees. She thought it was like a book, some brilliant and deeply American story. The green roll of hills, the white churches and tidy houses with their tidy lawns. And the town itself was laid out as neatly as a game board with straight streets, a small park and weathered brick buildings tucked in with faded clapboard.

She wanted to stroll those streets, wander the shops, watch the people as they went about their day. Perhaps have lunch in one of the little restaurants. Or better, she thought, stroll about with an ice-cream cone.

Del pulled into a parking lot. "Grocery store," he informed her as he dragged out his wallet. He pushed several bills into her hand. "Get what you need. I'll go check on your car. You've got thirty minutes."

"Oh, but couldn't we—"

"And get some cookies or something," he added along with a meaningful shove.

Eyes narrowed behind her shaded glasses, she climbed down, then stood with her hands on her hips as he pulled out of the lot again. The man was a complete blockhead. Ordering her, pushing her, cutting her off before she completed a sentence. She'd never been treated so rudely, so carelessly in her life.

It was beyond her comprehension why she enjoyed it.

Regardless, she'd be damned if she wouldn't see something of the town before he hauled her back to the cave for another week. Squaring her shoulders, she headed off to explore.

The pristine and practical New England village didn't run to pawnshops, but she did find a lovely jewelry store with a fine selection of estate pieces. And the earrings *were* tempting. Still, she controlled herself and earmarked the shop as a possibility for selling her watch should it become necessary.

She wandered into a drugstore. Though the choices of eye cream didn't include her usual brand, she settled for what she could get. She also picked up some very nice scented candles, a few bags of potpourri.

An antique store proved a treasure trove. It pained her to have to pass up the crystal-and-silver inkwell. It would've made a lovely gift for her uncle Alex— but was beyond her current budget unless she risked the credit card.

Still, she found some interesting old bottles for a reasonable price, and snapped them up. They'd be perfect for wildflowers and twigs, and would perk up the cabin considerably.

The clerk was a woman about Camilla's age, with dark blond hair worn in a sleek ponytail and sharp blue eyes that had noted her customer lingering over the inkwell. She smiled as she wrapped the bottles in protective paper.

"That inkwell's nineteenth century. It's a nice piece for a collector—at a good price."

"Yes, it's lovely. You have a very nice shop."

"We take a lot of pride in it. Visiting the area?"

"Yes."

"If you're staying at one of the registered B&B's, we offer a ten percent discount on purchases over a hundred dollars."

"Oh, well. No...no, I'm not." She glanced back to the desk where the inkwell was displayed. Her uncle's birthday was only three months away. "I wonder, would you take a small deposit to hold it for me?"

The clerk considered, giving Camilla a careful measure. "You could put twenty down. I'll hold it for you for two weeks."

"Thanks." Camilla took the bill from her dwindling supply.

"No problem." The clerk began to write out a receipt for the deposit. "Your name?"

"My...Breen."

"I'll put a hold tag on it for you, Miss Breen. You can come in anytime within the next two weeks with the balance."

Camilla fingered her watch, and a glance at it widened her eyes. "I'm late. Delaney's going to be furious."

"Delaney? Caine?"

"Yes. I was supposed to meet him five minutes ago." Camilla gathered her bags and rushed toward the door.

"Miss! Wait!" The clerk bolted after her. "Your receipt."

"Oh, sorry. He's just so easily annoyed."

"Yes, I know." The woman's eyes danced with a combination of laughter and curiosity. "We went out once or twice."

"Oh. I'm not sure if I should congratulate you or offer my sympathies." So she offered a smile. "I'm working for him, temporarily."

"In the cabin? Then I'll offer you *my* sympathies. Tell him Sarah Lattimer sends her best."

"I will. I have to run or I'll be hiking back to the cabin."

You got that right, Sarah mused as she watched Camilla dash away. Del wasn't a man known for his patience. Still, she sighed a little, remembering how she'd nearly convinced herself she could change him—tame him—when she'd been twenty.

She shook her head at the idea as she walked back to put the hold tag on the inkwell. She wished the pretty redhead plenty of luck. Funny, she thought now, the woman had looked familiar somehow. Like a movie star or celebrity or something.

Sarah shrugged. It would nag at her until she figured out just who Del's new assistant resembled. But she'd get it eventually.

Juggling bags, Camilla made it to the parking lot at a full run. She grimaced when she spotted the truck, then just wrenched open the door and shoved her purchases inside. "Have to pick up a few things," she said gaily. "I'll just be another minute."

Before he could open his mouth—to snarl, she was sure—she was rushing inside the market.

Snagging a cart, she set off toward produce at a smart pace. But the process of selecting fresh fruits and vegetables simply could not be rushed. She bagged lemons, delicately squeezed tomatoes, pursed her lips over the endive.

The supermarket was such a novelty for her, she lingered longer than she intended over fresh seafood, over the baked items. She liked the colors, the scents, the textures. The big bold signs announcing specials, and truly horrible canned music numbers playing over the loud speaker, interrupted only by voices calling for price checks and cleanups.

She shivered in frozen foods, deciding the chances of talking Del into an ice-cream cone now were nil. So she bought the makings for them. Delighted with the variety of choices, she loaded the cart, then wheeled it to checkout.

If she were a housewife, she thought, she would do this every week. It probably wouldn't be nearly as much fun. Just another obligation, she thought, and that was a shame.

She came back to reality with a thud when she moved up in line and saw her own face staring out from the cover of a tabloid.

Princess Camilla's Heartbreak

Why, they had her in grieving seclusion, Camilla saw with growing irritation. Over an aborted romance with a French actor. One she'd never even met! *Imbéciles! Menteurs!* What right did they have to tell lies about her personal life? Wasn't it enough to report every move she made, to use their telephoto lenses to snap pictures of her night and day?

She started to reach for the paper, for the sheer pleasure of ripping it to pieces.

"What the hell are you *doing* in here?" Del demanded.

She jumped like a thief, and instinctively whirled around to block the paper with her body. Fury, which she'd considered a healthy reaction, became a sick trembling in her stomach.

If she was unmasked here, now, it would all be

over. People would crowd around her, gawking. The media would be on her scent like hounds on a rabbit.

"I'm...waiting in line to pay."

"What is all this stuff?"

"Food." She worked up a smile as a cold sweat slid down her back.

"For what army?"

She glanced at the cart, winced. "I may have gotten a little carried away. I can put some of it back. Why don't you go outside and—"

"Just get through the damn line." He stepped forward, and certain he'd see the tabloid, she dug in her heels.

"Don't push me again."

"I'm not pushing you, I'm pushing the stupid cart."

When he moved past the newspaper rack without a glance, Camilla nearly went limp.

"Hey, Del, didn't expect to see you back in here so soon." The cashier began ringing up the things Del began pulling out of the cart and dumping on the conveyer belt.

"Neither did I."

The woman, a plump brunette whose name tag identified her as Joyce, winked at Camilla. "Don't let him scare you, honey. Bark's worse than his bite."

"Not so far," Camilla muttered, but was relieved that he was at the wrong angle now to see the grainy photograph of her. Still, she put her sunglasses back on before turning her face toward the cashier. "But he doesn't scare me."

"Glad to hear it. This one's always needed a woman with plenty of spine and sass to stand up to him. Nice to see you finally found one, Del."

"She just works for me."

"Uh-huh." Joyce winked at Camilla again. "You hear from your mom lately?"

"Couple weeks back. She's fine."

"You tell her I said hi—and that I'm keeping my eye on her boy." She rang up the total and had Camilla wincing again.

"I think I might need a little more money."

"Damn expensive lemons." Resigned, Del took what he'd given her, added more bills.

She helped him load the bags into the truck, then sat with her hands folded in her lap. She'd overreacted to the tabloid, she told herself. Still her initial spurt of anger had been liberating. Regardless, she'd recovered well, and a lot more quickly than she might have done just a week or two before.

That meant she was stronger, steadier. Didn't that serve to prove she was doing the right thing?

Now it was time to put that issue away again, and deal with the moment.

"I'm sorry I took so long, but I don't think it's unreasonable for me to want to see something of the town."

"Your car should be ready tomorrow. Maybe the next day seeing as Carl's claiming to be backed-up and overworked. Next time you want to play tourist, do it on your own time."

"Be sure I will. Sarah Lattimer at the antique store said to give you her best. I wonder that anyone so well-spoken and courteous could have ever gone out with you."

"She was young and stupid at the time."

"How fortunate for her that she matured and wised-up."

"You got that right." He caught her soft chuckle. "What's so funny?"

"It's hard to insult you when you agree with me." It was hard to brood about a silly photograph in a trashy newspaper when he was so much more interesting. "I like you."

"That makes you young and stupid, doesn't it?"

She grinned, then amused at both of them leaned over and kissed his cheek. "Apparently."

Chapter Six

I'm having the most wonderful time. It wasn't the plan to stay in one place so long, or to do one thing for any length of time. But it's such a beautiful place, and such an exciting thing to do.

Archaeology is truly fascinating. So much more interesting and layered to me than the history I enjoyed and was taught in school, or the sociology classes I took. More fascinating, I find, than anything I've studied or explored.

Who, where and why? How people lived, married, raised their children, treated their elderly. What they ate, how they cooked it. Their ceremonies and rituals. Oh, so much more. And all of it, society after society, tribe by tribe speaks, doesn't it, to our own?

He knows so much, and so much of what he knows is almost casual to him, in the way a true scholar can be. Not that knowledge itself is casual to him. He seeks it, every day. He wants to know.

I find that passion admirable, enviable. And I find it alluring.

I'm attracted to his mind, to all those complex angles. Working with—all right, for—him is hard and demanding, sometimes physically exhausting. Despite his injuries, the man has astounding stamina. It's impressive the way he can lose himself, hours at a go, in his work.

It's also an absolute thrill for me to do so as well. I've studied bone fragments that are centuries old. Sealed, of course, in plastic.

I wonder how they might feel in my hands. If anyone had told me I'd actually want to handle human bones, even two weeks ago, I'd have thought them mad.

How I wish I could go to the dig—or wet archeological site—and actually see the work being done there. Though Delaney paints a very clear picture when he speaks of it, it's not the same as seeing it for myself.

This is something I want to see, and do, for myself. I intend to look into classes, and what Delaney somewhat disdainfully refers to as knap-ins (a kind of camping session on sites for amateurs and students) when I'm home again.

I believe I've found an avocation that could become a vocation.

On a personal level, he's not as annoyed by me as he pretends to me. At least not half the time. It's odd and very educational to have someone treat me as he would anyone else—without that filter of manners and respect demanded by rank. Not that I appreciate rudeness, of course, but once you get to know the man, you can see beneath the rough exterior.

He's a genius. And though courtesy is never out of place, the brilliant among us are often less polished.

I find him so attractive. In my life I've never been so physically drawn to a man. It's exciting on one level, terribly frustrating on another. I was raised in a loving family, one which taught me that sex is not a game, but a joy—and a responsibility—to be shared with someone you care for. Someone you respect, and who affords you those same emotions. My position in the world adds another, complex and cautious layer, to that basic belief. I cannot risk taking a lover casually.

But I want him for a lover. I want to know what it's like to have that fire inside him burn through me. I want to know if mine can match it.

The tabloid in the supermarket reminded me of what I'd nearly let myself forget. What it's like to be watched, constantly. Pursued for an image on newsprint. Speculated about. The fatigue of that, the unease, the discomfort. Gauging how I feel now against how I felt the night I left Washington, I understand I was very close to breaking down in some way. I can look back and remember that hunted feeling, feel the nerves that had begun to dance, always, so very close to the surface.

Much of that is my own fault, I see now, for not giving myself more personal time to—well, decompress, I suppose—since Grand-père died, and everything else.

I'm doing so now, and none too soon.

My time here is, well, out of time, I suppose. I feel it's been well spent. I feel—perhaps renewed is an *exaggeration. Refreshed then, and more energized than I have felt in so many months.*

Before I leave and take up my duties again, I'll learn all I can about the science of archeology. Enough that I might, in some way, pursue it myself. I'll learn all I can about Camilla MacGee—separate from Camilla de Cordina.

And I might consider seducing the temperamental Dr. Delaney Caine.

The cabin smelled like a woodland meadow. Since it was a nice change from the musty gym sock aroma he'd gotten used to before Camilla, it was tough to complain.

And he wasn't running out of socks anymore. Or having to scavenge in the kitchen for a can of something for his dinner. His papers—after a few rounds of shouts and threats—were always exactly as he left them. A good third of his notes were typed, and the articles needed for the trade journals and the site's Web page were nearly finished. And they were good.

The coffee was always fresh, and so were the towels. And so, he thought with some admiration, was Camilla.

Not just the way she looked, or the pithy remarks that she aimed regularly in his direction, but her brain. He hadn't considered just how much a fresh mind could add to his outlook and his angle on the project.

He liked the way she sang in the mornings when she cooked breakfast. And how rosy she looked when she came out of the woods after one of her breaks. Breaks, he recalled, they'd negotiated with some bitterness.

He couldn't say he objected to the candles and

bowls of smelly stuff she'd set around the place. He didn't really mind the fancy soaps she'd put out in the bathroom, or coming across her little tubes and pots of creams in his medicine cabinet.

He'd only opened them for a sniff out of curiosity.

He even liked the way she curled up on the sofa in the evening with a glass of wine and grilled him about his work until he gave in and talked about it.

Alone in the kitchen, he did slow curls with a two-pound can of baked beans with his weak arm. It was coming back, he decided. And he was burning that damn sling. His muscles tended to throb at odd times, but he could live with that. Mostly it just felt so good to *move* his arm again. The ribs would take longer— the doctors had warned him about that. And the collarbone would probably trouble him for some time yet.

But he didn't feel so frustratingly helpless now.

Maybe he'd see if Camilla could give him a neck and shoulder massage, just to loosen things up. She had small hands, but they were capable. Besides, it was a good way to get them back on him again. She'd taken his orders to back off just a little more seriously than he discovered he'd wanted.

He paused, set down the can with a little thump. God, he was getting used to her, he realized with some horror. Getting used to having her around, and worse to *wanting* her around.

And that, he was sure, was the beginning of the end.

A man started wanting a woman around, then she expected him to be around. No more coming and going as you pleased, no more heading off to some dig for months on end without a concern about what you left back home.

Scowling, he looked around the kitchen again. Bottles of wildflowers, a bowl of fresh fruit, scrubbed counters and cookies in a glass jar.

The woman had snuck around and made the cabin a home instead of a place. You left a place whenever the hell you wanted. But home—when you left home it was always with a wrench.

When you left a woman, it was with a careless kiss and a wave. When you left *the* woman, he suspected it would rip you to pieces.

She came out of the woods as he thought of her, her face glowing, white wildflowers in her hand. How the devil had she come so close to becoming *the* woman? he asked himself with a spurt of panic.

They hadn't known each other for long. Had they? He ran a hand through his hair as he realized he'd lost track of time. What the hell day was it? How long had she been there? What in God's name was he going to do with himself when she left?

She came in, full of smiles. Well, he could fix that.

"You're late," he snapped at her.

Calmly she glanced at her watch. "No, I'm not. I am, in fact, two minutes early. I had a lovely walk, and fed the ducks who live on the pond." She moved over to the bottle, working her new flowers in with the old. "But it's clouding up. I think it's going to rain."

"I want to finish the section on brain tissue. I can't do if you're out feeding a bunch of ducks."

"Then we'll get started as soon as I pour us some lemonade."

"Don't placate me, sister."

"That would be beyond even my masterly capabilities. What's wrong, Del? Are you hurting?" She turned, the pitcher in her hand, and nearly bobbled it when she focused on him. "Your arm. You've taken off the sling." Quickly she set the pitcher aside and went to him, to run a hand along his arm.

He said nothing because, God help him, he wanted her to touch him.

"I suppose I expected it to be thin and wan. It's not." Her lips pursed as she tested the muscle. "A bit paler than the rest of you, and I imagine it feels odd and weak."

"It's all right. It just needs—ow!" The jolt made his eyes water when she pressed down firmly on his shoulder. "Hey, watch it, Miss de Sade."

"I'm sorry. Still tender?" More gently, she kneaded it. "You're all knotted up."

"So would you be if you'd had one arm strapped against you for the best part of two weeks."

"You're right, of course. Maybe some linament," she considered. "My mother would rub some on my father when he overdid. And I've helped treat some of the horses that way. I saw some witch hazel upstairs. After dinner, I can put some on your shoulder. Then you'll get a good night's sleep."

He had a feeling having her rub him—anywhere—wasn't going to insure quiet dreams. But he figured it was a good trade-off.

"Laboratory tests proved that the substance found inside the recovered skull was, indeed, human brain tissue. In total, during the three six-month field studies, preserved brain tissue was found in ninety-five of the recovered skulls. Twenty-eight contained complete brains, albeit shrunken to approximately a third of their normal size. The find is completely unique, with significant scientific impact and potential. This will give scientists a never-before possible opportunity to study brain matter which is more than seven thousand years old, with its hemispheres and convolutions intact. The DNA, the basic human building block, can be cloned from tissue older than any previously available."

"Cloned." Camilla's fingers stopped. "You want to clone one of the tribe."

"We can get into a debate on cloning later. But no, the purpose would be to study—disease, life expectancy, physical and intellectual potential. You can go back to your science fiction novel after we're done."

"They've cloned sheep," Camilla muttered.

He gave her a mild look behind the lenses of his reading glasses. "That's not my field. DNA research isn't my area. I'm just outlining the potential and import of the find. We have intact human brains, seven millenniums old. People thought with them, reacted with them. Developed language and motor skills. They used those brains to build their village, to hunt their food and prepare it. They used these minds to interact, to raise their children, to find a mate and for survival."

"What about their hearts?"

"What about them?"

"Didn't their hearts tell them how to tend their children—how to make those children in the first place?"

"One doesn't happen without the other, does it?" He took off the dark-framed glasses and tossed them aside. "These people cared for their young and had interpersonal relationships. But procreation is also an instinct—one of the most basic. Without young, there would be no one to care for the old, no replacement for the dead. There'd be no tribe. Man mates for the same reason he eats. He has to."

"That certainly takes the romance out of it."

"Romance is an invention, a tool, like..." He picked up the scarred head of an old, crudely fashioned hammer. "Like this."

"Romance is a human need, like companionship, like music."

"Those are luxuries. To survive we need food, water, shelter. And to insure continued survival, we need to procreate. Man—being man—came up with tools and means to make meeting those needs easier. And often more pleasant. And being man, he devised ways to make a profit from those needs, to compete for them, to steal for them. Even to kill for them."

She enjoyed him like this—enjoyed the casually lecturing mode when he discussed ideas with her as he might with a bright student. Or perhaps an associate. "That doesn't say much about man," she commented.

"On the contrary." He touched the jaw of a old, bleached-out skull. "It says man himself is a complex, ingenious and constantly evolving invention. He builds and destroys with nearly the same skill and enthusiasm. And is constantly remaking himself."

"So what have you made yourself?" she asked him.

He turned the hammer head over in his hand, then set it down again. "Hungry. When are we going to eat?"

* * *

She wasn't giving up on the discussion, but she didn't mind taking the time to think about it while she finished fixing dinner. She slid pasta into boiling water, tossed the salad. Sprinkled herbs on oil for the thick slices of bread.

She poured wine. Lighted candles.

And looking at the cozy kitchen, hearing the rain patter gently on the roof, she realized she had—unwittingly—employed a tool tonight. The scene she'd created was, unquestionably, a romantic one. She'd simply intended to make it attractive and comfortable. Instinct must have kicked in, she decided. Maybe for a certain type of person, particularly when that person was sexually attracted to another—creating romance was instinctive.

She found she liked knowing that about herself. Romance—to her thinking—was warm and generous. It took the other party's comfort and pleasure into account.

It was not, she decided as she drained the pasta, a damn hammer.

"A hammer," she declared to Del when he stepped in, "implies force or a threat."

"What?"

"A hammer," she said again, testily now. "Romance is not a hammer."

"Okay." He reached for a piece of bread and had his hand slapped aside for his trouble.

"Sit down first. Prove you've evolved into a civilized human being. And don't say okay just because you're bored with the subject and want to stuff your face."

"Getting pretty strict around here," he muttered.

"I'm saying that your tribe demonstrated human emotions. Compassion, love—hate certainly, as you did find remains that showed evidence of violent injury or death. Emotions make us human, don't they?" she demanded as she served the salad. "If it was only instinct that drove us, we wouldn't have art, music, even science. We wouldn't have progressed far enough that we'd build a village near a pond, create rituals to share and love enough that we'd bury our child with her toys."

"Okay. I mean okay," he insisted when she narrowed her eyes. He wanted the food in his belly and not dumped on his head. "It's a good point—and you could do an interesting paper on it, I imagine."

She blinked at him. "Really?"

"The field isn't cut-and-dried. It isn't only about facts and artifacts. There has to be room for speculations, for theory. For wonder. Edge over into anthropology and you're dealing with cultures. Out of cultures you get traditions. Traditions stem from necessity, superstition or some facet of emotion."

"Take our tribe." Mollified, she offered him the basket of bread. "How do you know a man didn't woo a woman by bringing her wildflowers, or a cup of fresh elderberries?"

"I don't. But I don't know that he did, either. No evidence either way."

"But don't you think there was a ritual of some sort? Isn't there always? Even with animals there's a mating dance, *oui?* So surely there had to be some courtship procedure."

"Sure." He dipped the bread, grinned at her. "Sometimes it just meant picking up a really big rock and beating some other sap over the head with it. Loser gets the concussion. Winner gets the girl.''

"Only because she either had no choice, or more likely, she understood that the man strong enough, passionate enough to smash his rival over the head to win her would protect her and the children they made together from harm."

"Exactly." Pleased with the tidy logic of her mind, he wagged a chunk of bread at her. "Sexual urge to procreation. Procreation to survival."

"In its own very primitive way, that's romantic. However, the remains you've studied to date don't show a high enough percentage of violent injury to support the theory that head bashing was this tribe's usual courtship ritual."

"That's good." Admiring the way she'd spun his example back to prove her point, he gestured with his fork. "And you're right."

"Del, do you think, eventually, there might be a way for me to visit the site?"

He frowned, thoughtfully now, as she served the pasta. "Why?"

"I'd like to see it firsthand."

"Well, you've got six months."

"What do you mean?"

"In six months if the articles and reports I'm putting together don't beat the right drum and shake out a couple million in grants, the site closes."

"Closes? You mean you'd be finished with the dig?"

"Finished?" He scooped up pasta. "Not by a long shot. But the state can't—or won't—allocate more funds. Bureaucrats," he muttered. "Not enough media attention after three seasons to keep them smiling for the cameras and handing over grants. The university's tapped out. There's enough private money for another six months. After that, we're shut down and that's it.''

The idea of the site closing was so appalling she couldn't get her mind around it. ''That can't be it if you're not done.''

''Money talks, sister.'' And he'd sunk all he could afford of his own into that dark peat.

''Then you'll get more. Anyone who reads your work will want to keep the project going. If not from the incredible archaeological significance of such amazingly rich findings, then for the completely unique scientific opportunities. I could—'' She broke off. She was an expert fund-raiser. People paid, and dearly, to see Princess Camilla at a charity function.

Media attention? That was never a problem.

More, she had connections. Her thoughts went instantly to her godmother, the former Christine Hamilton, now the wife of a United States senator from Texas. Both were avid supporters of arts and science.

''You got an extra million or so weighing you down, just pass it my way.'' Del reached for the wine bottle, stretching his healing shoulder a little too far, a little too fast. And cursed.

She snapped back to the moment. ''Be careful, you don't want to overtax yourself. I'm afraid I don't have a million on me.'' She smiled as she topped off his wineglass. ''But I have ideas. I'm very good with ideas. I'll think of something.''

''You do that.''

She let it go, and he forgot about it.

*   *   *

When dinner was finished, he vanished. It was a talent of his to disappear when dishes were involved. Camilla was forced to admire it. She couldn't claim the washing up pleased her nearly so much as making the mess in the first place.

Cooking was a kind of art. Washing dishes a mindless chore she'd have been happy to pass along to someone else.

In the cabin, however, she was the someone else.

In any case, she knew he wouldn't come near the back of the house until they were done. It gave her the opportunity to call home.

She kept one eye and one ear on the doorway while the connection to Virginia went through. Her youngest brother, Dorian, answered, and though normally she'd have been delighted to chat, to catch up on family news, to just hear his voice, she was pressed for time.

"I really need to talk to Mama."

"You take off like a gypsy, and now you can't give me the time of day."

"When I get back, I'll bore your ears off with everything I've done. I miss you, Dorian." She laughed quietly. "I never thought I'd actually say that, but I do. I miss all of you."

"But you're having a great time. I can hear it in your voice."

"I am."

"So you're not pining away for the French guy."

She huffed out a breath. Dorian considered teasing a royal duty. "I take back that I miss you. Where's Mama?"

"I'll get her. But I'd better warn you, she's got her

hands full keeping Dad from sending out a search-and-rescue. You're going to have to dance double-time to smooth things out with him.''

"I know it. I'm sorry, but I'm not a child."

"That's what Mama said. And he said—at the top of his lungs—that you were *his* child. Keep that in mind. Hang on.''

She knew he might tease, but Dorian was good as gold. He'd find a way to get their mother on the line without letting her father know.

Where would Mama be now? she wondered, and brought the image of the big, sprawling house in Virginia into her mind. In her sitting room perhaps. No, more likely out in the gardens, enjoying the evening.

Was it raining there, too?

Maybe she was entertaining. But no, Dorian would have said so.

As the silence on the line grew lengthy, Camilla began to fret.

Then she heard her mother's voice. "Camilla, I'm so glad you called. We were just talking about you."

"Is Daddy still very upset?"

"He's...adjusting. Slowly."

"I'm sorry, Mama. I just had to—"

"You don't have to explain to me. I remember what it's like. We just want to know you're safe, and happy."

"I'm both. I told you about the cabin, about Delaney. His work is so important, so interesting to me. Mama..." She reverted to French as English seemed too ordinary to explain her excitement in the project.

"You sound like a scientist," Gabriella laughed.

"I feel like a student. One who can't learn enough fast enough. Tonight I learned something distressing."

She explained about the project deadline as quickly as possible.

"That's difficult. Your professor must be very concerned."

"I'd like to help. I thought perhaps you could use your connections to find out what can be done, how much is needed. I was thinking—could you contact Aunt Christine? I'm good at raising money for causes, but she's even better. Finally I've found something that's really interesting—something that's personally important to me. I just need an idea of the right wallets to open."

"I can make some inquiries. Florida, is it? The Bardville Research Project, Dr. Delaney Caine. Give me a few days."

"Thanks. Thank you, Mama. You will be discreet? I'd just as soon he didn't know right now that Her Serene Highness Gabriella de Cordina had taken an interest in his work. It's so nice just being Camilla, I don't want to take a chance on anyone making the connection. Not just yet."

"Don't worry. The family's leaving for Cordina in a few days, Camilla. I'd hoped you might be ready to go with us."

"Another few weeks. Please. I'll contact you there and make arrangements to fly directly over when I...when I leave here."

"Take care of my baby. We love her."

"She loves you, too. I'll see you soon, Mama. I have so much to tell you."

After she hung up, Camilla hummed as she set the kitchen to rights. In so short a time, she thought, she'd accomplished much of what she'd set out to do. She was content with herself—and that had been something missing the past several months. She'd done ordinary things—too many of which had slipped away from her since adulthood.

And she realized much of that had been her own doing.

When she'd been a child, her parents had made certain she had a normal life, or as normal as possible. They'd done everything they could to keep her and her siblings out of the spotlight. But there had been duties, a gradual escalation of them as she'd grown.

Then the media had focused on her. Cordina's crown jewel, they'd dubbed her. And normality had begun to erode around the edges until the fabric of it was frayed. It had been flattering at first, exciting, even amusing. Then mildly annoying. After nearly a decade of constant attention, of speculative and outright fabricated articles, of being seen as a commodity, never as a human being, it had become smothering.

But now she could breathe again. And she knew she would go back to her life stronger, more capable and less vulnerable to the barrage.

She'd found a passion, and would now find a way to embrace it. This was the balance she'd seen and envied in her mother, in her aunts. Duty was never shirked, but each pursued a life full of interests and richness as a woman. So could she.

So *would* she.

One day she'd go on a dig and be part of a team that *discovered*. That sought knowledge and celebrated it. Let the media come, she thought as she prepared fresh coffee. The attention, while it lasted, would only generate interest in the field. And that meant funding.

It was unthinkable to allow their project to come to a premature end because of money. And it was their project now, she thought with a dreamy sigh. Hers and Delaney's. They shared it as they did the cabin, with each bringing their own stamp, their own mind, their own talents to the whole.

It was…marvelous.

Her excitement and passion might even be responsible for sparking the imagination of a generation of young women, bringing archaeology, the study of past peoples, cultures and customs into fashion.

She stopped, laughing at herself. Never satisfied with little steps, she thought. She always wanted more.

She filled two mugs and carried them into the living area. There he was, sitting on the horrible little sofa, his eyes intense behind his reading glasses, papers scattered over his lap and across the sprung cushions.

What leaped inside her was a wild and wonderful mixture of lust and longing, and, she discovered with a slow, warm sigh, love.

Why she was in love with him, she thought with surprise. Wasn't that…fascinating. Somewhere during this complicated and problematic interlude, she'd slid headlong into love with a bad-tempered, irritable, rough-mannered scientist who was more likely to snarl at her than smile.

He was rude, demanding, easily annoyed, impatient. And brilliant, passionate, reluctantly kind. It was a captivating mix that made him uniquely himself. She wouldn't change a single thing about him.

More, she thought, leaning against the wall to

watch him. He had one of the most essential traits she wanted in a friend, and in a lover. He had honor.

They were alone here, yet he'd never tried to take advantage of that. In fact, he rarely touched her even in the most casual way. Though he was attracted— she knew she wasn't wrong about that—his personal code wouldn't allow him to exploit the situation.

Her lips twitched in a smile. That made him, under it all, a gentleman. How he would hate to be termed so.

So, she was in love with an ill-tempered gentleman who wouldn't allow himself to seduce his temporary assistant. That meant it was going to be up to her to seduce him.

The idea, only an interesting fantasy until now, became more intriguing, more exciting now her heart was engaged. Love, she thought, gave her a marvelous advantage.

You're going to have to deal with me now, she decided. And you, Dr. Delaney Caine, don't have a prayer.

She nearly went back to the kitchen to exchange the coffee for wine. But she reasoned the caffeine would be more...stimulating.

The plan of attack should be simple. And subtle.

She walked to him, held out the coffee. "Which area has you snagged?"

"Huh?"

"Which area," she repeated, gesturing toward the scattered papers, "has you snagged?"

"I just need to think it through. Get this damn paperwork done. I need to get back to the site." He rolled his shoulder, testing it. "Into the lab."

She felt the quick hitch in her throat. If he was

starting to think about going back, she couldn't afford to be subtle for long.

Because when he went back, she intended to go with him. As his student, his associate. As his lover.

"The work you're doing here is just as important, just as essential. Though I'm sure it's not as rewarding for you."

"I'm not an administrator." He said it as though it were something foul, which made her smile.

"You'll soon be back in the field. You just need a little more time to finish here, and to heal."

He shifted, experimenting by stretching his torso. His ribs sang. An hour on the dig would have him crawling like a baby, he thought in disgust. But the lab...

"Let's get some of this down," he began, and rose too quickly. He had to grit his teeth as his body objected.

"Tell you what." Gently she took the coffee out of his hand. "I'll give you that rubdown first. It should help. You're always more uncomfortable first thing in the morning and after a long day. Let's loosen you up again. Then if you still want to work tonight, we'll work."

"I'm fine."

"You're not. And if you don't take care of yourself, you'll just delay your recovery and your return to the dig." Keeping her voice brisk, she started toward the stairs carrying both mugs. "Come on, we'll just consider it physical therapy."

He hurt, and that irritated him. He could take a pill—which would end up putting him to sleep and wasting work hours. He could put the damn sling back on, which would irritate him more. Or he could give the lubricant a try.

All he had to do was handle her rubbing her hands over him. And a man ought to have enough willpower to deal with that.

Besides, she had the coffee. He *had* to follow her upstairs.

"We can do it down here."

"Easier up here," she called back, smirking. "The sofa's a torture board, and too small in any case. No point in being uncomfortable. Just sit down on your bed. Take your shirt off."

Words, he thought, most men dreamed of hearing.

He wasn't going to think along those lines, he reminded himself. He was going to consider the entire experience a kind of therapeutic medicine.

Chapter Seven

She made a quick detour into her own bedroom and dabbed on perfume. Undid another two buttons of her shirt. If the man thought of romance as a tool, she was going in fully equipped.

She gathered the witch hazel, some fresh towels and some of the scented candles.

It was conniving, she admitted, but surely a woman in love was allowed some ploys. Just as, she thought as she stepped into his bedroom and saw every available light blazing, a wary man was allowed to try for some defense.

She found his safety precautions wonderfully sweet. And easily foiled.

"Let's have a look." She circled around the bed where he sat, then instantly lost her calculation in her sympathy. "Oh, Del, you really did a job on yourself, didn't you?"

"It's better."

"I'm sure, but..." The shoulder which had been hidden behind shirt or sling up till now was visibly swollen still. The bruising was a sickly yellow and green pattern that matched the clouds that ran along his ribs.

She wanted, more than anything else now, to simply nurse him, to ease his hurts.

"I didn't think about the swelling," she murmured, gently touching his shoulder.

"It's nearly gone." He moved his shoulder, as much to test it as to dislodge her hand. He wasn't, he realized, quite ready to have her touch him.

"Regardless. We should've been icing this down." Recalling what had happened before when she'd tried that particularly kind of medical attention had her pulse dancing.

She wanted to nurse him, and soothe. But that wasn't all she wanted, for either of them.

"Well, just relax, and we'll see what we can do about making you more...comfortable."

She turned away, started to arrange and to light the candles.

"What're you doing with those?"

The wariness in his voice had her lips curving. "Haven't you ever heard of aromatherapy? Just get as comfortable as you can, and we'll start on the shoulder first. You never told me how you were hurt."

"I was stupid enough to let some idiot kid drive from the lab. Some people just can't handle a wet road," he added with a bland stare. "He flipped the Jeep."

"Flipped?" Horror for him replaced any need to

defend her own driving skills. "My God, you're lucky you weren't killed."

"He walked away with a couple scratches," Del said bitterly. "He's lucky I didn't snap his neck like a twig. This has put me on the DL over three weeks already."

She walked over to turn off lights. "DL?"

"No baseball in your world, sister? Disabled list." He'd just think about baseball—sports were good—or work, or world politics. Anything but the way she looked in candlelight.

"How're you going to see if you turn off the lights?"

"I can see perfectly well. You won't relax with lights shining in your eyes." She wished he had a radio, a stereo system. Something. But they'd just have to cope without it.

She climbed onto the bed behind him, knelt.

The give of the mattress had his stomach muscles fumbling into knots—and his body bracing as if for battle.

"Now don't be stoic," she said. "Tell me if I hurt you. I'd say you're healing remarkably well if it's only been three weeks. And that you've carved through an impressive amount of work while you've been here."

She rubbed the lubricant in her hands to warm it, then began to gently stroke it over the bruises. "I think we can all use a change of routine now and again, to step away from what we've become steeped in so that we can have a clearer vision of the whole picture."

"Maybe." It was true enough that since he'd come back to the cabin he'd been able to look at the project from angles he'd missed or ignored when he'd been in the middle of it. Such as the money problem.

"Don't tense up," she murmured. "Just close your eyes." Her fingers stroked, gently kneaded. "Let your mind drift. Did you play in the woods here as a boy?"

"Sure." Baseball, he was going to think about baseball. How was he supposed to keep a box score in his head when she kept talking in that exotic, sexy voice.

"Swim in the pond? Fish?"

"My mother likes to fish."

"Really?"

Because the image of her, wearing one of her ugly hats, stout boots, ragged shirt and trousers with a pole in her hand made him smile, he closed his eyes.

Surely thinking of your mother was as good a way to control your glands as sports. Probably better.

"She never could get me or my father into it. Bores both of us crazy."

"I'm afraid I have the clichéd girl response to fishing," Camilla confessed. "Fish are slimy and they wriggle. I prefer them sautéed in a nice herbed butter. You don't have brothers, sisters?"

"No."

"Feel this knot here." She discovered one at the base of his neck. "You carry too much worry. That's why you're so irritable."

"I'm not irritable."

"No, you've a sunny disposition. Candy sweet."

"Ow."

"Sorry."

Oh, the man had a back, she thought with sheer delight. Broad and tanned with intriguing scars marring any hope of perfection. A warrior's back, she thought. Strong and male. She wanted, badly, to slide her lips down the length of it, nibble her way along the ridges. But it wasn't quite the time to abandon subtlety.

In any case, she wanted to help, wanted to ease his discomfort. Then jump him.

Distractions, she decided. As much for herself as for him. "The book there, the mystery novel? I've read that author before, but not that book. Is it good?"

"Yeah, it's not bad."

"You have a small selection of books here, but it's quite eclectic."

Okay, they'd talk literature, he decided. Talking was fine. Books instead of baseball. Same thing. "Novels can relax the mind, or stimulate it."

At the moment, he couldn't decide which she was doing to him. Her hands were like heaven. Soft and strong, soothing and arousing. His blood warmed despite his efforts to control it. Yet at the same time the aches and stiffness eased, bit by bit.

The scent of candles, the scent of her, the sound of her voice—low and soft as she spoke of books—relaxed him until his mind, as she'd ordered, began to drift.

He felt the bed give as she changed position, then that smooth glide of her fingers, her palm, on the front of his shoulder. Her breast brushed against his back, pressed cozily against him as she worked.

He wondered, dreamily now, how it would feel in his hand. Firm, small, smooth. How it would taste in his mouth. Warm and sweet and essentially female.

Her free hand moved to his other shoulder, kneading until tension melted away.

The rain pattered quietly on the roof, and the can-

dlelight flickered, warm and red against his closed
lids.

"Lie down." It was a murmur in his ear.

"Hmm?"

Her lips curved. Maybe he was a little too relaxed,
she thought. She didn't want him nodding off on her.
The more she touched him, the more she looked at
him, the more she wanted. Desire was a tightening
ball in her belly.

"Lie down," she repeated, and resisted—barely—
the urge to nip at his earlobe. She'd never in her life
craved the taste of flesh so much. "So I can reach."

His eyes blinked open, his mind tried to focus. Lying down wasn't a good idea. He started to say so,
but she was already nudging him back. And it felt so
good, so damn good to ease down.

"Your ribs are still a mess, aren't they? We'll get
to them. I suppose it's lucky you didn't break any."

"Yeah, it was my lucky day." He started to tell
her she'd done enough—God, he was so stirred up he
could barely keep two thoughts together—but when
she leaned over him, stretching out for the bottle
she'd set on the bedside table, those pretty breasts
blocked his vision. And then even those thoughts
scattered like ants.

"It would have been worse." She poured more lubricant into her palms, her eyes on his as she rubbed
it warm. "But you're in such good shape. You have
a strong, healthy body." She laid her palms on his
bruised ribs.

She was counting on the healthy part.

"How old are you, Delaney?"

"Thirty. No, thirty-one." How the hell was he supposed to remember when she was smiling down at him?

"Young. Strong. Healthy. Mmm." She sighed, and it wasn't all calculation as she carefully straddled him. "That's why you've made such a quick recovery."

He didn't feel recovered. He felt weak and stupid. Tension, of a much different sort, was pumping through him. She had her weight on her knees and was, slowly, rhythmically moving in a way that made him imagine her naked, made him imagine himself inside her.

He curled his fingers into fists before he reached up and just grabbed that tight, sexy bottom. "That's enough." His voice was a croak, a thin one. God help him.

She just kept her eyes on his. His had gone dark, gone hot. And his breath had quickened. "I haven't finished." She trailed fingers down to the waistband of his jeans, up again. And felt his stomach quiver. "There's a lot of you, isn't there? All hard and... tough."

He swore, but he couldn't work any venom into it. "Get off. You're killing me."

"Am I?" She only shifted. It was a very satisfying thing to hear the first time she set out, deliberately, to seduce a man. "I'll just kiss it, make it better."

Her gaze was a gold gleam under her lashes as she lowered her head, hesitated, then slowly rubbed her lips over his chest. She felt his heart kick like a stallion.

"Better?" She trailed her lips up his throat, over his jaw, then drew back, inches only when she heard him bite off a moan.

"This is nuts," he managed to say. "How long do

you expect me to keep my hands off you when you're climbing all over me?''

"Who said I expect you to keep them off me?" She closed her teeth lightly over his chin. "Who said I want you to? I think…'' She brushed her lips teasingly at the corner of his mouth. "I'm making it very clear what I expect. What I want."

"You're making a mistake."

"Maybe." She felt his hand grip her calf, then run firmly up to her thigh. And triumph lit her eyes. "So what?"

He couldn't come up with an answer, not when his system was screaming for her. He slid his hand over her hip until he could mold that lovely bottom. "You're taking advantage of me."

"I certainly am." She brought her mouth a breath closer. "Do you want me to stop? Now? Or do you want…'' She nipped her teeth teasingly into his lower lip, chewed gently, released. "More?"

Either way, it was probably going to kill him. But if he was going to die, he'd damn well die happy. "All or nothing."

"All then," she agreed and closed her mouth over his.

The first flash of heat stole his breath. It bolted through him, a lightning strike of power and electricity. He'd have sworn he felt every circuit in his brain fry.

The hand on her dug in reflexively, then clawed up to her back and fisted in her shirt. Impatient, nearly desperate, he yanked. And the jolt of pain had him swearing.

"No, no, let me. Just let me." She all but crooned it, running her lips over his face, his throat, bringing them back to his for a deep and drowning kiss. "I'm mad for your body."

His groan had nothing to do with pain as she ranged hot kisses over his chest, down to his belly and back again. Her low, humming sounds of approval seemed to vibrate from her and into him until he was trapped somewhere between pleasure and pain.

Aching to touch her he worked his hands between their bodies to find her breasts.

Breath unsteady, she sat back, shivered once. Then that slow female smile spread over her face. Watching him watching her, she reached for the buttons of her shirt, flipping them open one, by one, by one.

"I'm in charge this time," she told him and slowly peeled off the shirt. "You'll just have to lie there and take it."

"You got me up here for this, didn't you?"

She tilted her head, reached behind to unclasp her bra. "Yes. So?"

As the bra fell away and those lovely white breasts spilled out, he let out a long breath. "So. I appreciate it."

"Good. Touch me. I've spent hours at night wanting you to touch me."

He skimmed his fingers over her, saw her eyes cloud. "I wasn't going to let this happen."

"I wasn't going to give you any choice. Oh, *mon dieu, tes mains.*" His hands, his wonderful hands, big and strong and rough with calluses.

She was rose-petal soft, just as he'd imagined. He wanted to be gentle, careful with her. But he couldn't stop himself. And when she leaned over, bracing her weight on her arms, to mate her mouth with his again, his hands took more, took greedily.

He shifted, swore again as he fought against the protest of his ribs. "I need...I want..." His weight on her, his mouth on her. And though his side throbbed at the move, he managed to roll over.

"Wait. You'll hurt yourself."

"Shut up, shut up, shut up." Half mad for her, he scraped his teeth over the curve of her shoulder, breathed in her skin like a wolf scenting its mate. And had them both moaning when his mouth roamed down to her breast.

So hot, she thought as sensations battered her. His mouth, his skin, so hot against hers. As if they both raged with fever. His heartbeat was a gallop, and so was hers, as they raced to take more of each other. The weight of him was glorious, sinking her into the thin mattress and making her think of swimming beneath thunderous clouds.

To want and be wanted like this, for only herself, made her giddy and strong. And so very sure.

The thrill of it had her hands combing restlessly through his hair, digging urgently into his back as his muscles bunched.

Beneath them the bed creaked, overhead the rain drummed incessantly on the roof. Candlelight danced in the damp breeze that whispered through the open window.

And denim strained against denim as she arched beneath him. This time she quivered as he fought with the button of her jeans.

So soft, so tasty. And so ready, he thought, breathless as he fought her zipper down. She was already moving against him, those sexy little whimpers sounding in her throat. His mind was full of her, the scent, the shape, the flavor.

And he wanted more.

His fingers slid down, over the thin barrier of cotton, under it to the heat. Her whimpers became moans, and moans became quick, mindless gasps. When she erupted beneath him, he pressed his face to her belly and shuddered with her.

When his mouth roamed lower, she gripped the bedspread and prepared for the next onslaught on her senses. Her mind was hazed, her body a churning mass of needs and pleasures as sensations tumbled over and through her. It was staggering to *feel* so much, and still crave more.

He tugged the jeans over her hips, greedy for the next flash of flesh. And his bad shoulder gave out from under him. She let out a yelp of surprise when he collapsed on her. And while he cursed, violently, she began to laugh.

"It's all right, it's all right. *Merde!* My head's spinning. Let me help. Let me do it."

"Just a damn minute."

"I can't wait a minute." Still laughing, she wriggled, writhed and managed to drag herself free. Half naked and vibrating, she shoved and pulled until he rolled on his back again.

His face was fierce with frustration and temper, and only made her laugh harder.

"When I get my breath back, I'm going to whallop you."

"Yes, yes, I'm terrified." She scooted around on the bed, then had saliva pooling in his mouth as she wiggled out of the jeans. Temper, he admitted as she slipped off her panties, seemed a waste of time. Under the circumstances.

"Come back here."

"I intend to. But now." She reached over, unbuttoned his jeans. "Let's just get these out of the way. My hands are trembling," she said with a half laugh holding them out. "It's yours that have made them unsteady. I love the way they feel on me."

She yanked and tugged, pulling off jeans and shorts at the same time. Then her gaze roamed over him. Lingered.

"Oh. My." She drew in, then let out, a long breath. "Well, I did say there was a lot of you." Her eyes glinted with a combination of amusement and desire as she slid her body over his. "Put your hands on me again. Del, kiss me again."

"Bossy, aren't you?" But he cupped a hand at her nape and brought her mouth down to his.

She wallowed in the kiss, and it went slow and soft and deep. And when his hands moved over her, she felt the kiss edge over to urgent. "Tell me you want me," she murmured. "Say my name. Say my name and that you want me."

"Camilla." Her name echoed again and again in his head. "I want you."

She shifted, rose over him. And with her pulse pounding, took him inside her.

The first jolt of awareness had her bowing back. Holding, holding to absorb every drop of sensation until her system felt it might burst from the glory of it. His hands slid up her, closed over her breasts. Pressing her hands to his, she began to move. To rock. To push them both toward madness.

She was beautiful. He didn't know how to tell her.

Slim and white with that bloom of rose under the milk of her skin. Her hair was like a sleek cap of gold-shot fire. And the candlelight flickered, gold on gold, in eyes blurred with pleasure.

He couldn't breathe without breathing her.

He watched, unspeakably aroused, as she crested to another peak. And that long, lovely body pressed against his sparking sensation after sensation.

He wanted his arms around her, wanted to wrap them around her like chains. But he was pinned by his own injuries and the relentless demands of her body.

He fought to cling to reason another minute. Then one more. But his system screamed for the grand insanity of release. And his body plunged toward it, through it, as her head fell back on a low cry of triumph.

A cat, licking the last drop of a quart of cream from her whiskers, could not have felt more self-satisfied. That was Camilla's thought as she basked in the afterglow of lovemaking.

Everything about him, she decided, was completely delicious.

She wished she could stretch her body over his and just wallow. But he was lying so still, he might have been a dead man but for the regular sound of his breath.

She settled for slithering over to his good side and pressing a kiss on his shoulder. "Did I hurt you?"

He hurt, literally, everywhere. His bruises were throbbing like a nest of demons dancing under his skin. At the moment, pain and gratification were so mixed, he wasn't certain he'd ever be able to tell the difference. But he only grunted.

Arching eyebrows, she lifted herself on an elbow and stared down at his face. She should've helped him shave again, she mused. Though there'd been something oddly erotic about having that stubble rub over her naked skin.

He opened his eyes. "What?"

"You're trying to be annoyed this happened. It won't work."

Later, he decided, he'd think about if he were amused or uneasy that the woman read him so well. "Why not? I'm good at being annoyed."

"Yes, you should get an award. But you're going to want me again as soon as you've recovered, so you won't be able to be annoyed about it. Defeats the purpose."

"Awfully damn sure of yourself, aren't you?"

"About some things." She leaned down and kissed him. "About this."

"Well, it so happens, you're wrong, smart mouth." Because she was frowning at him, she didn't see the direction of his hand until it closed, possessively, over her breast. "I already want you again, and I might never recover from round one."

"I think you will. But I'm sorry you're hurting. I think I'll go down and make you an ice pack."

"I think you should settle down and be quiet for five minutes." To help her out, he pushed her elbow out from under her so her head bounced on his good shoulder.

"You have a body like a rock," she muttered.

"Don't try to get me going again, sister. I'm going to sleep for a half hour."

"Just let me—"

"Shh!" This time he solved the problem by wrapping an arm around her, and clamping a hand over her mouth.

She narrowed her eyes, considered biting. Before she could decide, his fingers went lax, his breathing evened out. She saw, to her astonishment, that he was as good as his word. He was, in ten seconds flat, sound asleep.

Thirty minutes later, shortly after she'd drifted from consternation into sleep herself, he woke her with a mind-numbing kiss. She shot to the surface, floundered there, then was dragged under again.

Later, when she lay sprawled on the bed, feeling dazed and used and gloriously ravished, he rolled over onto his good side, muttered something about blowing out the damn candles, and went instantly back to sleep.

For a long time after, Camilla stared up at the ceiling, grinning foolishly. She'd found another passion, she realized, and his name was Delaney Caine. The man she was going to marry, whether he liked it or not.

She was, as always, up before him in the morning. Routinely she brewed coffee, then decided to take the first cup with her on a walk to the pond. She felt Del deserved to sleep in.

They would, of course, have to juggle their time between Vermont, digs, Virginia and Cordina. It was going to make for a full, busy and, she thought, very rich life.

He'd like her family, and they him. After they got to know each other, she thought, nibbling on her lip.

She didn't suppose he'd care for the protocol and formality demanded by her duties to Cordina as a princess and niece to the king. But surely he could adjust there. Marriage was, after all, give and take.

Naturally she was going to have to convince him he wanted to marry her first. And before that she'd have to convince him he was in love with her.

He *had* to be in love with her. She couldn't have all this feeling inside her for someone who didn't return at least a part of it.

She wandered through the woods, watching the early sun slant quivering rays through the boughs. For now, she reminded herself, she would simply appreciate the moment. This time with him, and with herself, without a past or future. Time to enjoy the discoveries, the courtship and romance.

Just because she'd fallen in love quickly didn't obligate him to rush. And it didn't mean she couldn't drift a bit and savor the sensation of being a woman in love.

When she reached the pond, she sat on a stump. She'd have to see that they found a nice, weathered old bench to put here, she thought. And maybe she'd sink some containers of water lilies along the edge of the water.

Small changes, subtle ones, she mused. Nothing major. Just as she didn't intend to try to change anything vital and elemental where Del was concerned.

She'd put her mark on the cabin, hadn't she, while respecting its basic personality and charm. She would hardly afford the man less respect than she did his home.

No, she liked him the way he was. Her lips curved as she lifted the coffee cup. Just exactly as he was.

When they were both more accustomed to this new stage of their relationship, she'd find a way to tell him about her birthright. In another week, she decided. Surely she was entitled to one more week.

She'd have to find the right way to present things. She could start with her father, she mused. Casually mentioning that he'd once been a cop, and had gone into private security, buying the land in Virginia because he'd wanted to farm. How her paternal and maternal grandfathers had been friends. That was why, when her mother was in trouble, her grandfather had reached out to the son of his old friend for help.

A bit confusing, Camilla supposed, but it was a good start. Then she could say something like—oh, did I mention my mother's from Cordina?

That should, hopefully, open the door a bit wider. With any luck Del would comment, or have some minor question, so she could slide into a casual mention that her uncle, her mother's brother, was His Royal Highness Alexander de Cordina.

He'd probably laugh at that, say something like: *Sure, sister, and you're the queen of the May.*

She could laugh back, treating it all very lightly. *No, no, just a mere princess on a short, stolen holiday.*

And that, she decided, would never work.

She cursed in frustration, and in French, and propped her chin on her fist.

"You come all the way out here to swear at the ducks."

She yelped, spilling coffee onto the back of her hand. She sprang up and whirled to face Del. "I like it better when you clumped around like an elephant."

And he'd liked it better when he hadn't kept thinking how very beautiful she was.

He'd woken reaching for her. It seemed to him if the woman was going to slip into his bed, the least she could do was stay there. Then he'd panicked because she hadn't been in the house. The thought of her gone had sent him out in a rib-jarring run until he'd calmed himself down.

Now it was worse, a hundred times worse, because she wasn't gone. She was standing there, the sun and water at her back, looking like something out of a storybook.

The light played over that sleek cap of hair like jewels in a crown. Her eyes were more gold than brown, and seemed impossibly rich against the cool, clear skin. She had a half smile on her mouth—that long, lovely mouth.

He wanted, as he'd wanted the night before, to wrap his arms around her. To hold her exactly as she was.

And that was crazy.

"I didn't smell any breakfast."

"Because I haven't started it yet. I thought you'd sleep awhile longer."

"We said we'd start early today."

"So we did." Now she smiled fully. "I wasn't sure that still held, after last night." Since he wasn't coming to her, she stepped to him. Lifted a hand to brush at his hair. "How do you feel?"

"I'm okay. Listen, about last night…"

"Yes?" She rose on her toes, touched her lips lightly to his. And wound his stomach muscles into knots.

"We didn't lay out any of the... Look, there are no strings here."

A little bubble of temper rose to her throat, but she swallowed it. "Did I try to tie any on you while you slept?"

"I'm not saying—" He hated being made to feel defensive. "I just want us to be clear, since we didn't get into any of it last night. We enjoy each other, we'll keep it simple, and when it's over it's done."

"That's very clear." It would be undignified to strike him, and she didn't believe in resorting to physical violence. Particularly against the mentally deficient. Instead she smiled easily. "Then there's nothing to worry about, is there?"

With her expression pleasant, even patient, she ran her hands up his chest, lightly over his shoulders and into his hair. And fixed her mouth on his in a long, smoldering kiss.

She waited for his hand to fist in the back of her shirt, then nimbly stepped away and left him vibrating. "I'll fix omelets, then we'll get to work."

Her eyes sparked with temper and challenge as she started up the path. And smiled in the friendliest of manners as she turned, held out her hand.

Baboon, she thought—with some affection—as he took her hand to walk back to the cabin. You're in for one hell of a fight.

Chapter Eight

They had a week of relative peace. Camilla decided peace would always be relative when Delaney was involved. His grumpiness was just one of the things about him she'd come to count on. In fact, it was part of his charm.

She raided his books on archaeology. Though he muttered about her messing with his things, she knew he was pleased she had a sincere interest in the field.

When she asked questions, he answered them—and in more and more detail. It became routine for them to discuss what she had read. Even for him to suggest, offhandedly, another book or section she might want to study.

When he gave her a small Acheulean hand ax from his collection, she treasured the crude, ancient tool more than diamonds.

It was more than a gift, she thought. Much more than a token. It was, to her mind, a symbol.

He hardly complained at all about driving her back into town to pick up her car. And he took it for granted that whatever her plans had been before, mobile or not, she was staying awhile.

They were, Camilla thought, making progress.

She'd managed to peel a layer or two away as well. She learned his father was English, also Oxford educated, and had met his mother, an American, on a dig the senior Dr. Caine had headed in Montana.

So he'd spent some of his childhood in England, some in Vermont, and the bulk of it in trailers and tents on various sites all over the world.

The hand ax he'd given her was from Kent, and one he'd unearthed when he'd been a boy. It made the gift doubly precious to her.

He could read Sanskrit and Greek, and had once been bitten by a coral snake.

The scar just beneath his left shoulder blade was from a knife wielded by a drunk in a bar in Cairo.

However foolish it was, Camilla found all of this fabulously romantic.

She drove into town to mail off the first of his reports and correspondence. *Their* reports, she corrected, smugly. She'd contributed more than typing skills and he'd managed to indicate just that with a few approving grunts when she'd suggested a change or another angle of approach.

They made a good team.

When they made love, it seemed there was nothing and no one in the world but the two of them. Past, future were distant and irrelevant in that intense and eager present. She knew by the way he looked at her when they joined, the way his eyes would stay so vivid on hers, that it was the same for him.

None of the men who had touched her life had brought this kind of impact. To her heart, her body, her mind. She hoped—needed to know—that she brought the same to him.

No strings, she thought with a quick snort. Typical. If he wanted no strings why had he begun to take walks with her in the woods? Why did he answer patiently—well, patiently for him—when she asked questions?

Why did she sometimes catch him looking at her the way he did? So intense and direct, as if she were a puzzle he was trying to figure out?

And why did he, at the oddest moments, simply lean over and capture her mouth in a kiss that sizzled her brain?

The man was in love with her, and that was that. He was just too boneheaded to realize it. Or at least to admit it.

She'd give him a little more time, then she'd tell him she was in love with him. When he got used to the idea, she'd explain about the other part of her life.

It all seemed so reasonable as she ran her errands. Her mood was mellow when she strolled into the antique shop. She would try Sarah first regarding the watch, she decided. It was mortifying to be so low on cash, and have Del hand her money every time something was needed for the cabin.

Besides, if she could pay her way a bit more, she could fairly demand that he pull more weight on domestic chores. It was time he washed a few dishes.

"Good morning." She beamed a smile at Sarah as she wound her way through the antiques.

Sarah turned over the magazine she'd been paging through. "Good morning, ah...Miss Breen."

"I noticed you have a selection of secondhand jewelry and watches."

"Yes." Sarah answered cautiously as she studied Camilla's face.

"I wonder if you'd be interested in this." Camilla took off her watch, held it out.

"It's lovely. Um..." Hesitantly Sarah turned the watch over. She ran her fingers over the smooth gold, watched the tiny diamonds wink. "It's not the sort of thing we usually..."

She trailed off, then simply stared at Camilla.

"It's all right. I thought I'd see if you might be interested in buying it. I'll try the jeweler."

"You are her." Sarah barely breathed it, her eyes wide and dazzled.

There was a hard clutching in Camilla's throat, but her face remained perfectly calm. "I beg your pardon?"

"I thought...when you were in the other day...I knew you looked like somebody."

"Everyone looks like someone." With a steady hand, Camilla reached for her watch. "Thank you anyway."

"Princess Camilla." Sarah pressed her fingertips to her lips. "I can't believe it. Princess Camilla, in my shop. You're right here. And, and here!" Triumphantly now, she flipped the magazine over.

And there, Camilla saw with a sinking heart, was her own face being touted as one of the most beautiful in the world.

"You cut your hair. All that fabulous hair."

"Yes, well." Resigned, Camilla sighed. "It was time for a change."

"You look wonderful. Even better than—" Catching herself, Sarah paled. "Oh. Excuse me. Um. Your Highness." She dipped in a quick curtsy that had her blond tail of hair bouncing.

"Don't. Please." Struggling to smile, Camilla glanced toward the door and prayed no other customers would come in. "I'm traveling very quietly at the moment. I'd really prefer keeping it that way."

"I taped that documentary on the royal family. After you were in last week, I kept thinking and thinking, and then it hit me. I watched it again. But I thought I had to be wrong. Cordina's Crown Jewel doesn't just drop in to my store for old bottles. But here you are."

"Yes, here I am. Sarah—"

"That Del." Overwhelmed Sarah babbled on. "I know you have to pry news out of him with a crowbar, but this is taking it too far. He's got royalty staying at his cabin, and he doesn't say a word."

"He doesn't know. And I'd prefer to keep things that way as well, at least until… Oh, Sarah."

Having a princess in her shop was one thing, having one who looked so miserably distressed was another. "Golly." Biting her lip, Sarah hurried around the counter, but stopped short of taking Camilla's arm. She didn't think it was done. "Would you like something to drink, Your Highness?"

"Yes. Yes, thank you, I would."

"I've got, jeez, I'm so flustered. I have some iced tea in my office."

"That's very kind of you."

"It's nothing. Just let me, boy…I'll put the Closed sign on."

She hurried to the door and back again, then wrung her hands and couldn't stop herself from doing another curtsy. "Behind the counter. It's not much."

"I'd love something cool." She followed Sarah into the little office and took a seat on a swivel chair while Sarah fumbled with the door of a small refrigerator. "Please don't be nervous. I'm no different than I was the first time I came in."

"I beg your pardon, Your Highness, but you are. Of course you are."

"You needn't address me by my title," Camilla said wearily. "Madam or ma'am is sufficient, and in this case, I'd prefer you just use my name."

"I don't think I can. You see I've read about you and your family since I was a kid. We're almost the same age, and I used to imagine myself living in a palace, wearing all those beautiful clothes. Being a princess. I guess most little girls do."

She turned back to Camilla, eyes shining. "Is it wonderful?"

"It can be. Sarah, I have a great favor to ask you."

"Anything. Anything at all."

"Would you not tell anyone?"

Sarah blinked. "Anyone? At all?"

"Just for a little while. Please. Sarah, it can be wonderful being a princess, but there were times, you see, when I was a little girl, that I dreamed of being just that. Just an ordinary girl. I want time now to live that dream."

"Really?" It sounded beautifully romantic. "I guess we always want what we don't have." She handed Camilla a glass of iced tea. "I won't tell anyone. It'll kill me,'' she admitted with a wry laugh. ''But I won't. Could you, would you mind, ah, madam, signing my magazine?''

''I'd be happy to. Thank you very much.''

''You're nicer than I thought you'd be. I always imagined princesses would be, well, snobby.''

''Oh, we can be.'' Camilla smiled, sipped. ''Depending.''

''Maybe, but, excuse me, but you seem so…normal.''

The smile warmed, as did her eyes. ''That's the nicest thing you could say to me.''

''Classier of course. I noticed that right off, too, but…'' Sarah's eyes popped wide again. ''Del doesn't *know*?''

Guilt circled, nibbled at the back of her neck. ''It hasn't come up.''

''It's just like him. Oblivious.'' Sarah threw up her hands. ''The man's oblivious. When we were dating, I think he forgot my name half the time. And forget noticing the color of my eyes. Used to make me so mad. Then he'd smile at me, or say something to make me laugh, and I wouldn't mind so much.''

''I know what you mean.''

''He's so smart about some things, and so lame about others.'' She picked up her own glass, then nearly bobbled it when she caught the dreamy expression on Camilla's face. ''Holy cow. Are you in love with him?''

''Yes, I am. And I need a little more time to convince him he likes the idea.''

It was just like a movie, Sarah thought. ''That's nice. Really nice. And it's perfect, really, when you think about it.''

"It is for me." Camilla admitted, then rose. "I'm in your debt, Sarah, and I won't forget it." When she held out a hand, Sarah quickly wiped her own on her slacks before taking it.

"I'm glad to help."

"I'll come in and see you again before I leave," Camilla promised as she started back into the shop.

When she picked up her watch from the counter, Sarah bit her lip again. "Your Highness, ma'am, do you really want to sell that watch?"

"Yes, actually. I'm embarrassingly short of liquid funds, just now."

"I can't give you what it's worth, not even close. But I could...I could lend you five hundred. And, well, you could have the inkwell you liked so much."

Camilla looked over at her. The woman, she thought, was nervous, intimidated and confused. But it didn't stop her from wanting to help. Another gift, Camilla thought, she would treasure.

"When I started out on this quest of mine, I wanted to discover... To find parts of myself as well as see...I'm not sure what now—maybe just things from a different perspective. It's such a wonderful bonus to have found a friend. Take the watch. We'll consider it a trade, between friends."

Del walked out on the front porch and stared at the rutted lane. Again. How long did it take to run a few errands? That was the trouble with women. They turned a couple errands into some sort of pilgrimage.

He wanted his lunch, and a fresh pot of coffee, and to answer the half-dozen e-mails that had come through his laptop that morning.

All of which, he was forced to admit he could handle for himself. Had always handled for himself.

What he wanted, damn it, was her.

His life, he thought jamming his hands into his pockets, was completely screwed. She'd messed everything up, scattered his focus, ruined his routine.

He should've left her stranded in the rain that night. Then everything would be the way it had been before. He wouldn't have some woman cluttering up his space. Cluttering up his mind.

Who the hell was she? There were secrets tucked inside that sharp, complicated brain of hers. If she was in trouble, why didn't she just tell him, so he could deal with it?

He needed for her to tell him, to confide in him, to depend on him to help her.

And when the hell had he started seeing himself as some knight on a white charger? It was ridiculous, totally out of character.

But he wanted to fix whatever was wrong. More, he realized, much more, he needed her to trust him enough to tell him. Trust him enough to fix it.

Because he'd tripped over his own unspoken rule and fallen flat on his face in love with her.

And he didn't much care for the way it felt, he mused, rubbing a hand over his heart. It was a lot more uncomfortable than a few bruised ribs. And, he feared, a lot more permanent.

He'd had to go and say no strings, hadn't he? Of course, she'd had no problem with that, he thought now. Bitterly. That was just fine and dandy with her.

Well, if he was going to have to adjust, then so was she.

Besides, no strings didn't mean no faith, did it? If

she didn't believe in him enough to even tell him her full name, where were they?

He paced into the house, then back out again.

Maybe he should go check on her. She'd been gone nearly two hours. She'd already had one accident, which meant she could easily have another. She might be sprawled over the wheel of her car, bleeding. Or...

Just as he was working himself into a fine state of agitation, he heard the sound of her engine. Disgusted with himself, he slipped back into the house before she could catch him keeping an eye out for her.

He circled the living room twice, then paused and considered. Adjustments.

Romance.

That was something she appeared to believe was vital in any culture. Cultures were made up of relationships, rituals and romance. Maybe he should try a small foray into that and see where it got him.

He strolled into the kitchen as she set a bag of groceries on the table. "I have your receipts for the overnight mail I sent," she told him.

"Good." Since he wanted to anyway, he brushed a hand over her hair.

She gave him an absent smile, and turned away to put a quart of milk in the refrigerator. "There were some letters in your post office box." Frowning, she rubbed at her temple where a tension headache nagged. "I must have left them in the car."

"No problem." He leaned down to sniff the side of her neck. "You smell great."

"I what? Oh." She patted his shoulder, reached for the bag of new potatoes she'd bought for dinner. "Thank you."

Determined to make an impression he dug a little

deeper. What was it women always…ah! "Have you lost weight?" he asked, feeling truly inspired.

"I doubt it. Probably gained a couple if anything." She took coffee out of the cupboard and prepared to brew a fresh pot.

Behind her back, Del narrowed his eyes. Since words weren't getting him anywhere, he'd move straight to deeds.

He scooped her off her feet and started out of the kitchen.

"What are you doing?"

"Taking you to bed."

"Well, really. You might ask—and I haven't finished putting the groceries away."

Del paused at the bottom of the steps and stopped her mouth with his. "In certain cultures," he said when he eased back, "women indicate their desire for intimacy by stocking the pantry. I'm merely picking up on traditional signals."

Amusement nudged at the gnawing worry inside her. "What cultures?" she demanded as he continued up the steps.

"Mine. It's a new tradition."

"That's so cute." She nuzzled at the side of his throat. "I think you missed me."

"Missed you? Did you go somewhere?" When she huffed out a breath, he tossed her on the bed. When she bounced, he rolled his shoulder. "Got a twinge from hauling you up. Maybe you have gained a couple pounds."

She shoved herself up on her elbows. "Oh, really?"

"That's okay. We'll work it off." And he dived on her.

Her first reaction was laughter. Playfulness wasn't his usual style, and it caught her off guard. As he rolled her over the bed, she forgot to be worried.

"You're heavy." She shoved at him. "And you haven't shaved. You have your boots on my clean linens."

"Nag, nag, nag," he said, and dragging her hands over her head, took her mouth with his.

He felt her pulse jump, then race, and her hands go limp in his. Her body gloriously pliant.

He skimmed his lips over her jaw. "You were saying?"

"Shut up and kiss me."

He cuffed her wrists with one hand, used the other to unbutton her shirt. "So, are you indicating your desire for intimacy?" He trailed a fingertip down the center of her body, toyed with the hook of her slacks as he watched her face. "Just want to get my signals straight."

Her breath was already backing up in her lungs. "Your pantry's been stocked since I got here, hasn't it?"

"That's a good point." He lowered the zipper, brushing his knuckles over the exposed skin. "Had the hots for me all along, haven't you?"

"If you're going to be arrogant—"

"Maybe you were hoping I'd come into your room one night," he continued, and traced the dip between her center and her thigh. "And do this."

"I never…" Her hips arched, her breath hissed out as he cupped her. "Lord. Del."

"Let me show you what I thought about doing."

Keeping her hands pinned, he touched her, unerringly shooting her up into an intense climax, muffling her shocked cry with his mouth as her body bucked. When her breath sobbed, he closed his teeth over her breast, torturing the sensitized point through the cotton of her bra.

He nudged the straps down, nibbled his way over the slope of her shoulders, almost delicately, while his hand roamed, exploited and plundered.

She went wet and wild beneath him. Unable to find her balance, she shuddered, then spiked, then floated down again only to have him fling her ruthlessly over the edge one more time. Her hands strained against his grip. And the helplessness added a layer of panicked excitement over shattered senses.

Her body was molten, and she trembled from the heat that slathered her skin and burned in the blood. Still she arched to him, desperate for more.

She heard his voice, the words thick and soft.

"I'll owe you for this," he said and snapped the bra in two with one rough tug.

Then his mouth, his teeth, his tongue, found flesh. The moan wrenched from her gut as her system erupted.

"Let me go. Let go of my hands. I need to touch you."

"Not yet, not yet." It would end too soon if she touched him now. He hadn't known he could arouse himself to a frenzy just by arousing her. He wanted her weak and wrecked and wailing.

And he wanted to take, take, take.

When he felt her go fluid beneath him, when he felt release pour through her and leave her lax, it still wasn't enough.

He tore the panties away, feeling a dark satisfaction

at hearing the delicate fabric rip. Then he drove her back to madness with his mouth.

Finally, when she thought there could be no more, he filled her. Her hands slipped off his damp shoulders, her mouth lifted urgently to his.

And she wrapped herself around him like a vine.

"Mon amour. Mon coeur," she murmured mindlessly as they tumbled over the brink. *"Toujours mon amour."*

They slept, sprawled over each other like exhausted children. And when they woke, steamed the walls in his narrow shower as they took each other again under the hot spray.

Realizing he was taking an unprecedented step—a day off—Camilla packed a picnic and cajoled him into sharing a very late lunch by the pond.

She didn't have to do much cajoling. Picnics, he thought, were romantic. And romance was the current name of the game.

She looked happy, he mused. Relaxed. Her face glowed, her eyes were soft. If he'd been an artist, he'd have painted her now and titled it Camilla Content.

He didn't feel foolish—or not very—telling her so.

"That's just what I am. I love this place." She stretched out on the bank, stared up at the powder-puff clouds. "It's so quiet, it seems as though there's no one else in the world." She turned her head to smile at him. "Perfect for a hermit."

"I'm not a hermit." He polished off the last of the fancy triangular shaped sandwiches she'd put together. "I just don't like people around."

"I like people." She rolled onto her stomach. "They're often so much kinder than you expect," she added, thinking of Sarah. "But sometimes, if you don't have a place to be alone—or to be quiet—you forget that and only see the demands, the responsibilities, the obligations people mete out."

"If you don't have a place to be alone, you don't get anything done."

"You have such purpose, your own purpose. That's a gift. Not everyone does." Her eyes clouded. "Some of us fumble around looking for one, and end up with so many we realize, all at once, we haven't got any at all."

"You don't strike me as a fumbler."

"Hmm. Sometimes efficiency is just as much of a flaw. Without that quiet time, you stop seeing the flaws, and the virtues. You can forget, not just who you are, but who you want to be." She smiled up at him, then turned over again to rest her head on his lap. "So I like this spot, because it's helped me remember."

"And who are you, Camilla?"

She understood he wanted an answer—a real one. But she found she couldn't speak and irrevocably change this moment. So she evaded. "A woman who won't forget again." She picked up a plum, took a bite, then held it up to him. "I like being alone with you, Delaney."

And she would give them the rest of the lovely, lazy day before Camilla de Cordina joined them.

He wanted to be patient, but patience wasn't his best skill. He'd thought, been sure, she'd been ready to confide in him. What did a man have to do to pry that woman open? he wondered. Most people spilled their guts at the least provocation.

But she just made vague philosophical statements, an occasional wistful one. And clammed up.

It was grating, but he was going to have to press. To do that he was going to have to make it clear that they were...that he was...

He'd never in his life told a woman he loved her. He'd gotten through his entire adult life without it being an issue, much less a problem. Now it was both.

He could march into the kitchen and blurt it out and be done with it. He equated it to ripping off a bandage in one painful jerk. Or he could ease them both into it, stage by stage—like lowering yourself into a cold pool inch by inch so your body adjusted to the shock.

I like having you around, he could say. Maybe you should just plan on staying.

He could let that settle awhile then move up to the I-care-about-you level. She'd have something to say about that. She *always* had something to say. Who would have believed he'd like listening to her so much?

But in any case, he thought, drawing himself back to the point, when they'd finished hashing through all that, he could just finish it off.

"I love you." He winced at his own muttered voice, shot a look toward the kitchen. It didn't even *sound* like him, he decided. The words didn't seem to fit his mouth.

"I love you," he tried again, and exhaled. Easier that time.

"Now, tell me what kind of trouble you're in, I'll take care of it and we'll move on."

Simple, he decided. Direct and supportive. Women liked supportive.

God. He was going to need a good shot of whiskey to get through it.

"I know it's late." Cocking the receiver on her shoulder, Camilla looked down at her wrist before she remembered her watch was gone. A quick glance at the kitchen clock had her calculating that it was after one in the morning in Cordina. No wonder she'd woken Marian.

"No problem. I was only sleeping."

"I'm sorry. Really. I just had to tell someone."

"Okay, let me pull myself together. Are you coming home?"

"Soon. I promise."

"You missed the first fitting for your ball gown. Your dressmaker is seriously displeased."

"Ball gown?" She drew a blank before it clicked in. "Oh, the Autumn Ball. There's plenty of time. Marian, I'm in love."

"You say that now, but if you'd heard the woman gnashing her teeth, you'd…what? What?"

"I'm in love. It's wonderful. It's terrifying. It's the most incredible thing that's ever happened to me. He's perfect. Oh, he's the most irritating man half the time, but I *like* that. And he's so smart and so funny— and very committed to his work."

"Camilla."

"And he's very attractive. I know that's just surface, but isn't it nice to fall in love with the inner man and have the outer man be gorgeous?"

"Camilla."

"He's in love with me, too. He's coming around to that, though it might take just a little while longer to—"

"Camilla!"

"Yes?"

"Who is he?"

"Oh, he's the man I've been working for here. Delaney Caine."

"The archaeologist? You fell for Indiana Jones?"

"I'm serious, Marian."

"Well, does he at least look like Indiana Jones?"

"No. Hmm, actually perhaps a little. But that's not the point. This isn't a game or a movie, it's my life. And this is something I want, something that feels very right."

"I can hear that. Cam, I'm so happy for you. When will I meet him?"

"I don't know exactly." Gnawing over the question, she wrapped the phone cord around her fingers. "That's part of the problem. After I explain things, then I hope we can make arrangements for him to meet the family."

"Explain things?" There was a long pause. "You mean you haven't told him who you are?"

"Not yet. I didn't expect this to happen, did I? I couldn't anticipate it. And then I wanted..." She trailed off warily as she heard Del heading into the kitchen.

"Camilla, how could you let things go so far and not tell him? If the man's in love with you—"

"I don't know that," she murmured in French. "Not for certain. I didn't intend for it to be complicated."

She cleared her throat as Del took the whiskey bottle from the pantry. It wasn't possible to ask him to hurry, or to cut Marian off, so she continued the conversation in French, keeping her voice as mild as she could manage.

"Marian, I had a right to my privacy. I could hardly stay here, if I'd announced I was a member of the royal family. The whole point of this was not to be Camilla de Cordina for a few weeks."

"The point seems to have changed."

"Yes, I know that, but I'd hardly be staying here if people knew who I was. The cabin would be surrounded by the media, and that, if you recall, was what sent me off in the first place."

"If you think the man would call reporters—"

"No. No, of course I don't think that. And I didn't call to argue with you, Marian. I did what I had to do, what I thought best, for me. As to the rest." She slanted a look toward Del as he poured whiskey into a glass. "I'll deal with it."

"I'm your friend, Camilla. I love you. I just don't want to see you hurt or disappointed. Or exploited."

"I don't intend to be. Tell the family I'll be home soon."

"And your dressmaker?"

Camilla sighed. "Inform Madam Monique that Her Highness will not disgrace her at the Autumn Ball. Go back to sleep, Marian."

She hung up, opened the refrigerator for a cold drink while Del stood swirling his whiskey in the glass. "I hope you don't mind me using the phone."

"No, I don't mind."

"I reversed the charges."

"Good. I'd probably have gotten a jolt if I'd noticed a call to Cordina on my phone bill next month."

"Yes, I imagine so. I..." She trailed off, and the hand that had lifted for a glass fell to her side again.

"Je parle francais aussi." Del lifted the whiskey to his lips as she turned to face him. "Your Highness."

Chapter Nine

She knew her color faded. She could feel it drain and leave her face cold and stiff. Just as she could feel her heart leap into her throat and fill it with pounding.

Because of it she instinctively straightened her spine.

"I see. You didn't mention it."

"Must've slipped my mind," he said evenly. "Like being a member of the royal family of Cordina slipped yours. Just one of those stray details."

"My lineage never slips my mind. It isn't allowed to. Delaney—"

"So what's all this?" He gestured with the glass. "Your little version of the princess and the pauper? Taking a few weeks, slumming with the hoi polloi."

"You know better. You can't think that."

"Let's see, what should I think?" He lifted the

whiskey again, splashed more in the glass. He couldn't precisely pinpoint why he wanted to heave the bottle against the wall. Or more, why he resisted. "What, are you hiding out from a lover? One a little too anxious to get his hands on the crown jewels?"

"That's unfair. I have no lover but you."

"Not for the past couple of weeks anyway. You should've told me I was having sex with a princess. It might've added a nice flair."

Her lips wanted to tremble, so she firmed them into a hard line. "And that's unkind."

"You want fair? You want kind?" His voice changed from dangerously soft to viciously sharp. "You've got the wrong guy, sister. Somebody plays me for a fool, I get pissed."

"I didn't play you. I never intended to—"

"To what? Cut the crap, Camilla. You don't do anything you don't intend. You came in here because you wanted to play pretend for a while, and amuse yourself with the locals while you were at it."

"That's not true." Her temper started to build to match his. "And it insults both of us."

"You're insulted." He slammed the glass down before he did throw it. "You come into my place and pretend to be someone you're not. You lie about who you are. About what you are. Virginia farm girl, my ass."

"My father has a farm in Virginia." She shouted back because she was too frightened to do otherwise. "I've lived there half the year all of my life."

"And the other half in the palace. Well, I guess the tiara suits you better than a straw hat."

"Yes. No!" Struggling through the anger and

panic, she dragged a hand through her hair. "We have a farm in Cordina. My mother—"

"Your 'French' mother," he said coolly.

"You said France, I said Europe." But it was weak, and she knew it. "Delaney, I'm exactly the same person I was ten minutes ago. I only wanted the privacy of—"

"Privacy? Give me a break. You slept with me. You made damn certain you'd sleep with me. What, looking for a change of pace from the purebreds? You get points for nailing stray Americans on your little adventure?"

Her color came up now, flaming into her cheek. "How dare you! You're crude and vile, and it's despicable to turn something lovely into something cheap. I won't have this discussion, nor explain myself to you while you're in this impossible mood. Move aside."

"You don't give commands here, Princess." He grabbed her arm before she could stalk by him. "You used me."

"No." Tears wanted to brim, wanted to fall. "Not the way you mean. Del, I only wanted a place to be. I only wanted some time."

"You got a hell of a lot more, didn't you? Playtime's over, Your Highness. You're going to do more than explain yourself."

"Let me go." She drew on all of her composure and command, and eyed him coldly. "I have nothing more to say to you now. Let me go."

"Oh, I will. All the way. I guess we've said all there is. You can pack your bags and run away, since that seems to be your pattern."

The temper and shame that warred within her were no match for the grief. "You want me to go?"

"You got what you came for, didn't you? I'll make it easy for you and get the hell out of your way."

Her breath hitched as he started for the door. "Del. Please, don't. I love you."

The pain stabbed through him. The words snarled out of him as he tossed them at her, though they were pure truth. "You're breaking my heart, sister," he said, "try that line on someone who's stupid enough to believe it. And get the hell away from me." He left and slammed the door behind him.

He tromped through the forest for an hour, thinking vicious thoughts and cursing all women. He stalked the woods another hour as the flames of his temper banked to a smoldering rage.

In love with him? What a crock. She had a lot of nerve pulling that routine on him. She'd been about to pour on the tears, too. He'd seen that coming. Thank God he'd gotten out of there before the floods hit.

He just couldn't stand weeping females.

Well, she'd pulled every other trick out of her hat. Excuse me, he thought bitterly, make that crown. Why not tears?

And for what? So she could have a couple weeks to indulge herself. Cinderella in the wilderness?

He stopped, rubbing at the ache in his gut as he stared out over the pond.

I love this place.

He could hear her saying it, see the easy pleasure in her face as she lay on the grass beside him.

So she had an appreciation of nature. Big deal.

Haven't you ever needed to just breathe?

He remembered her saying that, too. That first day, standing beside him with all that tension in her face, in her voice. As if she'd been standing on the edge of something and fighting to hold her ground instead of leaping over.

Okay, so maybe she had some problems. Who didn't? But that didn't excuse what she'd done. It had all been a pretense, right from the beginning. And she'd let him fall in love with her—let him fall into that cage without warning him it had a trap door to nowhere.

She had to pay for that.

He turned, headed back toward the cabin. Okay, he'd let her explain—not that he was buying any of it. Then…

Then he'd figure out what the hell to do next.

With his head down and his hands in his pockets, he didn't notice her car was gone until he was nearly at the back door. For nearly a full minute he stared blankly at the spot where it had last been parked.

Then he was bolting into the cabin, charging up the stairs.

Her clothes were gone. He flung open both closets as if she might have put them back in the spare room just to make him sweat. She'd even taken the pots and tubes from the medicine cabinet.

On a tearing fury, he searched the cabin for a note. But there was nothing.

He couldn't say she'd gone without a trace. She'd left the candles, the little bottles springing with wild-flowers. Her scent, everywhere, was already haunting him.

So, she'd pulled up stakes, he thought. Just because

he'd yelled at her and told her she could pack and run away. If the woman couldn't stand up to a fight...

No, better this way, he reminded himself. No point in dragging it out. She was heading back to where she belonged to where she'd been headed all along, and he could get back to work without having her distract him every five minutes.

He prowled over to his notes, picked up one at random. After tossing it down again, he dropped onto the couch to brood.

She'd come back. He talked himself into that, particularly when he got just a little drunk. She was just off in a snit, that was all. Women had snits, didn't they?

His two hours stomping through the woods was a natural expression of justifiable aggravation. He didn't go off in snits.

In the morning, suffering from a surprisingly nasty hangover, he convinced himself he didn't want her to come back. He liked his life the way it had been before she'd plunged into it. And he didn't like, not one damn bit, this sensation of loss and misery. Which was, no question about it, completely her fault.

By the second day, he was edgy and busily working himself into a temper again. She had absolutely no business running off before he'd finished yelling at her. But it was just like her, wasn't it, to stick that chin out, shoot that nose in the air and flounce off. He should've recognized it as princess behavior from the get-go.

When she cooled off and came back, he had a great deal to say to her.

Why the hell hadn't she come back?

Didn't matter to him, he reminded himself and struggled to concentrate on his work. He had plenty to do to keep himself occupied while she was off sulking. In fact, maybe he'd just pack up and take himself back to the dig. It was where he belonged anyway.

And it gave him a hard, rude jolt to realize he'd planned to take her with him. He'd wanted to show her the place, to watch that interest and intellect shine in her eyes when she got her first look at his pet project.

He'd wanted to share that with her—and that was terrifying. He'd wanted to share everything with her. He couldn't believe how much that hurt.

Just as he sat, unsteady in the knowledge that she really wasn't coming back, he heard a car coming down the lane.

He *knew* it! He sprang up, fueled with relief, pleasure, and fury, and had reached the door in one leap before he stopped himself. This was not the way to handle it, he decided, or her. He'd *wander* out, casually. Then he'd let her apologize.

Feeling smug, and generous, he stepped outside. Everything inside him sank when he saw it wasn't Camilla climbing out of the car. It was his parents.

"Surprise!" Alice Caine ran toward the porch in her ancient and sturdy boots. Her hair, a streaky mess of mouse-brown and gray was, as always falling untidily from beneath a scarred bush hat. She was trim as a girl, with a face splattered with freckles and lined from a life in the sun.

She leaped on her son, gave him a slurpy, smacking kiss on the cheek, then immediately turned to her husband. "Niles, let the boy get the bags. What's the point in having a big, strong son if you can't use him as slave labor? How's the shoulder, Del?'' she asked him. ''And the rest of it?''

''Fine. It's fine. I wasn't expecting you.''

''If you had been, it wouldn't be a surprise.'' She tipped down her dark, wire-rim glasses. Though she grinned, she was sharp enough to have seen her son's shocked disappointment when he'd stepped out on the sagging porch. ''Got some coffee?''

''Sure. Sure.'' Ashamed of himself, he bent down—she was such a little thing—and gave her a quick hug.

''Drove three hundred, fifteen miles today.'' Mumbling in his public school English accent, Niles Caine finished noting the mileage in his tattered book as he crossed to his son. ''Made good time.''

He was a big man, tall and dashingly handsome at sixty-seven. His hair, a mop of it, had gone shining silver, and his eyes, green as his son's, were jewel sharp in his tanned face. He tucked the book into the pocket of his faded shirt, then gave Del a crushing bear hug. ''How's the shoulder?''

''Fine. Better. What's up with your dig?''

''Oh, we're just taking a break. Clear the mind.'' Alice said it airily, one warning look at her husband, as she strode into the house. She stopped dead, fisted her hands on her narrow hips. ''Del. You've got a woman.''

''What?''

''Look at this. Flowers.'' She arched her brow at the wildflowers tucked into bottles. ''Scents,'' she added, sniffing a bowl of potpourri. ''Clean.'' She ran a fingertip over a tabletop. ''Definitely a female on the premises. Where is she?''

"She's not here."

Ah, Alice thought. Poor baby. "Niles, my hero, would you run into town and get me some ice cream?"

"Run into town?" He stared at her. "I've just got here. I haven't so much as sat down yet."

"You can sit down in the car on the drive to town."

"Woman, if you wanted ice cream, why didn't you say so when we were still in the bloody car?"

"I didn't want any then. Something with chocolate." She rose on her toes to kiss his scowling mouth. "I've such a yen for chocolate."

"Flighty, fluttering females," he muttered, and stomped back out to the car.

Alice simply walked to the couch, sat and propped her boots on the table. Smiling, she patted the cushion beside her. "Sit. Coffee can wait. Tell me about the woman."

"There's nothing to tell. She was here, she was a constant annoyance. Now she's gone."

Cranky, wounded bear, she thought indulgently. Just like his father. "Sit." Her voice firmed—she knew how to handle her men. "Why did she leave you?"

"She didn't leave me." His pride pricked, he dropped onto the couch. "She was just working for me, temporarily. Very temporarily," he muttered.

And at his mother's long, patient silence, he cracked. "I kicked her out. If she's too stubborn to come back...I don't need her underfoot anyway."

"There now." She patted his head. "Tell Mommy all about the horrible girl."

"Cut it out." But his lips twitched.

"Was she ugly?"

"No."

"Stupid then."

He sighed. "No."

"A cheap floozy."

Now he laughed. "Mom."

"That's it then." She slapped a hand on his thigh. "A cheap floozy taking advantage of my poor, sweet-natured, naive little boy. Why, I'll fix her wagon. What's her name? I'll hunt her down like a dog."

"She's fairly easy to find," he murmured. "Her name's Camilla. Her Royal Highness Camilla de Cordina. I could strangle her."

Alice tossed her sunglasses and her hat on the table. "Tell me," she said. So he did.

She listened while he worked himself back and forth through temper, into misery and back into temper again. So often, she noted, he had to leap up to pace the room just to keep up with himself.

His description of Camilla—except for the irritating, interfering nuisance portion—jibed with the lovely note she'd received some days before from Her Serene Highness Gabriella.

A gracious—and clever—note, Alice mused, one that acknowledged Gabriella's gratitude to Delaney for his hospitality to her daughter. Alice hadn't been sure if having anyone consider her son hospitable was more of a surprise than learning he was being so with a member of Cordina's royal family.

But she was a woman accustomed to thinking on her feet, and adjusting in midstride when necessary. The contents of the note had caused Alice to drag her husband from the Arizona dig and head home to see for herself just what was what.

Now that she'd seen, she had a very good idea just what was what.

What came through, in huge, neon letters to her mother's view, was that her son was completely, pitifully in love.

And it was about damn time.

"So she left," Del finished. "That's for the best all around."

"Probably so," Alice agreed calmly. "It was short-sighted of her to deceive you. Certainly she should've felt comfortable—frankly even obliged—to be forthcoming with you after you told her your own lineage."

"Huh?"

"Obviously a viscount is lower in rank—considerably—from a princess, but she should've had the courtesy to trust you as you trusted her." Delighted by her son's blank face, Alice crossed her booted feet at the ankle. "You did tell her your father is Earl of Brigston—and you are Viscount Brigston."

"It didn't come up," Delaney said, then added with more heat "Why would I?" as his mother simply watched him coolly. "Who remembers anyway? I never use it."

Unless it suits you, Alice thought. But it was enough, she decided, that she'd planted that little seed. "There's your father, back with the ice cream. Let's have some with our coffee."

She gave her son a day, partly because she simply enjoyed him, and partly because she knew he had to chew on things. She debated how she'd tell him she'd been in communication with Camilla's mother.

"He might get his back up all over again," she

mused as she cast her line into the pond. "It would be so like him." At her husband's grunt, she turned to where he sat, papers scattered over his lap and the ground. "Pay attention, Niles."

"Hmm? What? Damn it, Alice, I'm working."

"Your son's work."

"Just leave him alone. A man should handle his own affairs without any interference."

"Hah. So you said to me thirty-three years ago this coming winter. Look where it got you."

"Got me you, didn't it?"

She grinned out over the water. Two peas in a pod, she decided. Her men were two very stubborn peas.

Before she could decide how best to handle things, the matter was taken out of her hands. Del swooped through the woods, making enough racket to scare away every fish for ten miles, and scooped her right off her feet.

"We've got new funding."

"Good thing, because we're not getting any fish for dinner." Still she hugged him. "That's wonderful, Del. Who?"

"I don't have the details—just got the call from the university. I've got to get back to the dig. Sorry to run out on you like this."

"Don't be." She tucked her tongue in her cheek. She saw how it would work now. Perfectly. "Give us a call once you're settled."

"Will. Have to pack."

That evening, while her son was—very likely— steaming over the idea that his funding was being generated by the interest and influence of a young princess, Alice sat and composed a tidy and formal note to Her Serene Highness Gabriella de Cordina.

The Earl and Countess of Brigston, along with their son, Lord Delaney, Viscount of Brigston, were very pleased to accept her gracious invitation to the Autumn Ball in Cordina.

"It's insulting." Camilla waved the latest communication from Del. "Rude and insulting and just like him."

Gabriella sat calmly, fixing simple pearls at her ears. Guests who had been invited to stay at the palace for a time before and after the ball, would be arriving shortly. "It sounded perfectly polite and informative to me, darling."

And she found it very telling that in the month she'd been back in Cordina her daughter had lost none of the heat where Delaney Caine was concerned.

"That's because you don't know him," Camilla raged on. "Insufferable is what it is. Reporting to me as if I were some sort of accountant. Dollars and cents, that's all. He doesn't tell me anything about the finds—the things he'd know I'd want to know. And see how he signs them? Dr. Delaney Caine. As if we were strangers. He's detestable."

"So you've said." Gabriella turned on the chair of her dressing table. Her hair was swept back from a face her husband told her grew more lovely with each year.

She didn't believe him, but it was nice to hear. Her eyes, the same tawny gold as her daughter's were quietly sober and showed none of the humor and anticipation she felt.

"I'm sure he's grateful for your help in funding the

project, Camilla. You parted on such bad terms, he
probably feels awkward as well.''

"He should feel awkward. He should feel sorry and
small." She whirled around her mother's lovely
room. Stared out the window at the stunning view of
the gardens, the bright blue sea beyond. "I didn't get
the funding for him in any case. I got it for the project. The work's the priority. It's an important find and
it deserves to be completed.''

And her daughter's interest in the work hadn't
waned in the weeks since she'd been back. If anything, Gabriella reflected, it had increased. She'd
spent hours with books, had gone to the university to
speak to professors who were knowledgeable, had
raided their library for more books and documents on
archaeology.

She'd neglected none of her duties. It simply
wasn't in Camilla's makeup to do so. There were
times Gabriella wished she were less dedicated. Even
though she'd been worried, she'd been pleased when
Camilla had taken those weeks for herself.

Her own heart had hurt when her little girl had
come home with hers broken. She was grateful their
relationship was such that Camilla had confided in
her. About falling in love—and becoming Delaney's
lover. It helped a woman, Gabriella knew, to talk to
a woman.

And now, though she knew her daughter suffered,
part of her rejoiced that Camilla's heart was constant.
She was still very much in love. Her mother, with a
little help, intended to see she got what she wanted.
Even if it meant a little—very little, she assured herself—finagling.

She rose, crossing to her daughter to lay her hands

on her shoulders, a kiss on the back of her head. "Love isn't always polite."

"He doesn't love me." Camilla hurt still, sharply. "Mama, he looked at me with such contempt, turned me out of his life with less compassion than you would a stray dog."

And should answer for it, Gabriella thought fiercely. She was counting on her daughter to see that he did. "You weren't honest with him."

"I was trying to be honest with myself. If I was wrong, there still should've been room for... It doesn't matter." She straightened her shoulders. "I have my interests and duties, and he has his. I wish this ball were over and done."

"When it is, you'll go on your first dig. It'll be exciting for you."

"My mind's full of it." Ruthlessly she folded Del's formal letter, set it aside. As she would, she promised herself, set thoughts of him aside. "Imagine me, studying artifacts from the Lower Paleolithic in France. Dr. Lesuer has been so generous, so forthcoming. I'll enjoy working with his team and learning from him. But now, I'm behind schedule. Sarah Lattimer will be here in a couple hours. I believe I told you about Sarah—the shop keeper from Vermont who was so kind to me?"

"Yes, you did. I'm looking forward to meeting her."

"I want her to have a spectacular time. Aunt Eve's going to give her a tour and she'll have a chance to meet Uncle Alex before the ladies tea tomorrow."

"I need you to greet some of my personal guests with me—the Earl and Countess of Brigston and their

son. They should be here within thirty minutes. I'm
entertaining them in the Gold Parlor on arrival.''

"Yes, I remember." She glanced at her watch. "I
don't suppose you could have Adrienne fill in for
me."

"Your sister's in the nursery with young Armand
and the baby. I won't keep you above fifteen
minutes,'' Gabriella promised.

"I'll be there. I'll just adjust a few things in my
schedule." She started out, came back and picked up
Del's letter. "I need to have this filed,'' she murmured, and hurried away.

Exactly twenty-nine minutes later, Camilla dashed
down the main staircase. Preparations for the Autumn
Ball—and all the events leading up to and following
it—were well underway. The *regisseur,* the palace
manager, would overlook no details. And should he,
her aunt's eagle eye would scope them out.

Her Royal Highness, Princess Eve de Cordina was
Chatelaine of the palace, and a woman who stood
beside her husband as he ruled the country. But she
often had her own opinions about matters of state,
and had her own career apart from her royal duties.
Her Hamilton Company of players was a world-
renowned theatrical group and she was also a respected playwright.

Her example served to remind Camilla that with
ambition, work and brains, a woman could do anything. Even be on time—barely—to meet guests when
her plate was overfull.

She was nearly at the base of the steps when the
man jogging up to her caught her by the shoulders.
He was handsome as sin and smelled comfortably of
horses.

"What's the hurry?"

"Uncle Bennett. I didn't even know you'd arrived." She kissed her mother's youngest brother on the cheek. "And already visited the stables."

"Bry and Thadd are still out there," he said, referring to his two young sons. "Hannah's around here somewhere. She wanted to talk to Eve. And look at you." He ruffled her short hair. "Very chic."

"How was your trip to England?"

"Successful. I found the perfect mare to breed with my stallion."

"I want to see her and all the rest of you—but later. I'm late."

"What's this about some American who needs a good ass-kicking?"

She rolled her eyes. "You've already seen my father."

"On the way in from the stables. I volunteered to hold his coat."

"I don't think you'll have the chance. I don't see the ass he'd like to kick being within striking distance any time in the near future. *A bientôt.*"

"But—" Puzzled, Bennett watched her dash off. Someone had their information skewed, he mused, then began to smile as he climbed up the steps, hoping to search out his brother and harass him for details.

Knowing Reeve MacGee, Bennett doubted that Camilla's father had the wrong data.

Camilla slowed to a dignified if brisk walk as she moved through the palace. Flowers, fresh and elaborate, speared and spilled out of vases and urns. Her heels clicked efficiently on the sparkling marble floors.

The occasional servant paused to bow or curtsy. She greeted most by name, but continued on. She hated being late.

By the time she made it to the Gold Parlor, she was. By six minutes. Because she heard the low murmur of voices, she took another moment to smooth her skirt, her hair, take a breath and fix a welcoming smile on her face.

When she stepped in, she saw her mother was already seated in one of the conversation areas, pouring tea from one of the Miessen china pots into cups for a middle-aged couple.

The woman caught her attention first. Such an intriguing look, Camilla thought. Lovely in a unique way, and casually disheveled. She wouldn't have called the baggy tweeds fashionable, but they certainly suited the woman.

The man rose as she approached. She started to speak, to apologize for her tardiness in greeting them. Then couldn't speak at all. He was, she thought, stunned, an older and more distinguished version of Del.

She needed to find a way to get the man off her mind, she ordered herself, when she started seeing pieces of him in dashing and dignified English earls.

"Camilla, I'd like to introduce you to the Earl and Countess of Brigston. Lord and Lady Brigston, my daughter, Her Royal Highness Camilla de Cordina."

"Lord and Lady Brigston, I apologize for not being here with my mother to welcome you to Cordina. Please, sit and be comfortable. I hope you enjoyed your trip."

"We're delighted to be here, Your Highness." Alice smiled as she curtseyed, then shook hands with

Camilla. "As is our son. May I present Lord Delaney, Viscount Brigston."

Her thoughts whirled as Del moved from the far window and crossed the room toward her. Her heart beat too quickly—first with the sheer joy of seeing him, and then with confusion. And lastly, with anger.

Viscount Brigston, she thought. What was this? How did the American scientist become a British aristocrat? The nerve of him.

She inclined her head, coolly, then lifted her chin. "My Lord," she said in a tone frigid as winter.

"Madam," he returned, and with annoyance clear in his eyes, took her offered hand and kissed it.

She got through it. Camilla was too proud, and too innately well mannered not to. But the following thirty minutes were torture. She held up her part in conversation. Which was more, she thought darkly, than Del managed. He barely grumbled monosyllables, and only when directly addressed.

Why did he have to look so big and handsome and *male?* The suit and tie should have dwarfed him somehow, or tamed him by a few degrees. It did neither.

"My son," Alice said at one point, "is delighted and grateful for your assistance in funding the Bardville Project, madam. Isn't that right, Del?"

He shifted in his chair. "I've relayed my appreciation, and the team's, to Her Highness via letters and reports."

"Yes, I received one of your…letters just this morning, Lord Delaney." Camilla smiled with her eyes frosted. "How odd you didn't mention you'd be traveling, and so soon, to Cordina."

He wouldn't have been here if he'd had any choice, he thought. His mother had hounded him like a she-wolf and all but dragged him to the plane by his ear. ''I wasn't entirely sure my schedule would permit the trip.''

''We're so pleased it did,'' Gabriella broke in, warned by the battle-light in her daughter's eyes. When Camilla's temper rose too high, her tongue could be lethal. And rash. ''So that we can, in some small way, repay you for the hospitality you offered Camilla in your home in Vermont. A lovely part of America, I'm told. I regret never having seen it for myself.''

It was a toss-up, Gabriella decided, who looked more shocked by her easy mention of their prior relationship, the princess or the viscount.

Both gaped at her while she sipped her tea. She thought—was nearly certain—she heard the countess muffle a squeak of laughter.

Now, she would see how long the two of them could manage to continue to behave like polite strangers.

''Camilla has developed a keen interest in your field, my lord,'' Gabriella continued. ''It's always rewarding for a mother to see her child so enthusiastic.''

''And equally rewarding for a child to entertain her mother,'' Camilla said with a perfectly pleasant smile—one with an edge only her mother could see. ''What an…interesting surprise for you to have invited Lord Delaney and his parents without mentioning the plans to me.''

''I hoped it would be, and that you'd be pleased to

offer Cordinian hospitality." It was said lightly, but with underlying firmness.

"Of course. Nothing could please me more than repaying Lord Delaney for...everything."

"I'm sure you'd like to rest a bit after your journey," Gabriella said to Niles and Alice as she rose. "Camilla, perhaps you could show Lord Delaney the gardens."

"I'm not—" Del began, then ground his teeth at his mother's killing glare. "I wouldn't want to put you out."

"It's no trouble at all." Gabriella laid a hand, a heavy one, on Camilla's shoulder as she passed.

Trapped, Camilla got to her feet, braced herself as her mother breezily led Del's parents away then turned to face him. "First, let me make it perfectly clear that I had no idea you would be here, and if I had I would have done everything possible to be absent from this welcoming party."

"That's clear. If I could've gotten out of making this trip, I would have. Believe me."

"Second," she continued in the same cool and mannered tone, "I have no more desire to show you the gardens than you have to see them. However, I've less desire to distress my mother or your parents. Ten minutes should do it. I'm sure we can tolerate each other for that length of time. My Lord," she said in a hiss.

"Don't start on me." He rose as well, then found himself talking to her back as she strode to the terrace doors on the other side of the room.

When she sailed out, he jammed his hands into his pockets and followed. It was going to be, he thought, a very long four days.

Chapter Ten

In the third floor guest wing, Alice paused at the entrance to the suite of rooms they'd been given for their stay in Cordina.

It was time, she decided, to test her impressions and instincts regarding Gabriella de Cordina.

"I wonder, ma'am, if I might have a moment of your time. In private."

"Of course." Gabriella had been calculating her options and considering how best to handle her guest since she'd first set eyes on the woman. In her opinion, Alice Caine preferred the direct approach. And so, when possible, did she. "We'll use my sitting room. It's very comfortable, very private."

As she led Alice through the palace, to the family quarters, she spoke of the history of the building, the art collection. She kept up the polite tour chatter until they were comfortably behind closed doors in her elegant rose and blue sitting room.

"May I offer you some refreshment, Lady Brigston?"

"No, ma'am, thank you." Alice took a seat, folded her hands. "We are, obviously, both aware of the relationship between our children, and the unfortunate way that relationship was left late last summer," she began.

"Yes. Your son was very kind to provide my daughter with shelter."

"I beg your pardon, but that's nonsense. He didn't do it out of kindness, or at least only partially. He isn't unkind, he's just boneheaded."

Gabriella sat back. "Lady Brigston…Alice," she responded warmly, pleased that her judgment about the woman had been on target. "I wasn't certain I was doing the right thing for Camilla by inviting your family—and by not telling her of the invitation or about your son's title. It was self-serving of me. I wanted to give her time to search her heart, and I wanted to gauge her reaction for myself when she saw your son again. The minute I did, I knew I'd done the right thing after all."

"You saw the way they looked at each other—well, before their backs went up."

"Yes, I did. They love each other, and they're both letting pride get in the way."

"It's more than pride with Del. He's so much like his father. Toss him some old bones, and he can give you chapter and verse on the woman who owned them three thousand years ago. Give him a flesh and blood female, and he's clueless. It's not that he's stupid, ma'am—"

"Brie," Gabriella interrupted.

Alice took a breath, settled more comfortably in the chair. Like her son, she knew the formalities of protocol—and like her son found them mildly foolish. She was glad Her Serene Highness felt the same way. "Brie. He's not stupid. He's just a Caine. Through and through."

"I don't like to interfere in the lives of my children," Gabriella began.

"Neither do I. Technically."

They said nothing for a moment, then both began to smile. "Why don't we have a small glass of brandy," Gabriella suggested.

It helped, Alice thought, when you could see the woman your son loved in her mother's eyes. And you liked them both. "Oh, why don't we?"

Pleased, Gabriella rose to fetch the decanter and pour the snifters herself. "I do have an idea, which while not—technically—interfering, may help things along a bit. My sons would call it double-teaming."

"I'm all ears."

Ten minutes later, Alice nodded. "I like your style. Good thing, since we're going to be in-laws." She glanced toward the window when she heard raised voices. "That's Del—booms like a bull when he's mad."

They rose together, moved out to the balcony. In tune they linked arms as they looked down on their children. "They're arguing," Gabriella said with emotion thickening her voice.

"It's great, isn't it?"

"We shouldn't eavesdrop."

"We're just standing here, taking some air. We can't help it if they're shouting at each other."

"I suppose not."

Even as she inched out a bit more, Gabriella heard her sitting room door open and slam shut.

"Is that jackass Caine here yet?"

Mortified, Gabriella closed her eyes, then turned back as her husband came to the open doorway. "Reeve," she murmured.

"You must be Camilla's father." Delighted, Alice stepped forward, pumped his hand. "I'm the jackass's mother. We were just pretending not to eavesdrop while they yell at each other in the garden. Care to join us?"

He stared, a tall man with silver shot black hair, as his wife began to laugh helplessly. "Well, hell," was all he said.

She hadn't intended to argue. In fact, Camilla had ordered herself not to rise to any bait he might cast. The jackass. She swept him along garden paths as if they were on a forced march, and took none of the pleasure she normally did in the scents, the textures, the charm.

"We're particularly proud of our rose garden. There are more than fifty varieties represented, including the climbing specimens trained on the fifteen arbors in what is called *La Promenade de Rose*. The less formal beds at the far edges add charm, I think, to elegance."

"I don't give a hang about the roses."

"Very well, we'll continue on to the walled garden. It's a particularly lovely spot where—"

"Let's just cut it out." He took her arm, pulled her around.

"I have not given you leave to touch me, sir."

"Tell that to somebody who hasn't seen you naked."

Her color came up—fire under cream—but her voice remained cold. "Nor do I care to be reminded of my previous poor judgment."

"Is that what it comes down to, poor judgment on your part?"

"You're the one who ended it."

"You're the one who took off."

"You told me to go!"

"Like you ever listened to a damn thing I said. If you'd been honest with me from the beginning—"

"You dare?" Incensed, she yanked her arm free. "Honesty, *Lord* Delaney?"

He had the grace to flush. "That has nothing to do with anything. I didn't tell you I had chicken pox when I was ten, either, and it's just as relevant."

"Your title is hardly a rash."

"It's just a title, something I inherited from my father. It doesn't—"

"Ah! Titles, lineages, don't count when they're yours, only when their mine. You asinine jerk."

"Just watch it. Just watch it," he ordered. "It's not the same, and you know it. I don't think of myself that way. I don't use the damn thing, and don't remember it's there half the time. I don't live in a palace and—"

"Neither do I! I live on a farm! This is my uncle's home. You say you don't think of your title half the time. I have no choice but to think of mine every day—with every public move, and most private ones. I wanted time, a little time to live as you live, to have what you take for granted. Freedom. So I took it," she said passionately. "Right or wrong, I took what I needed because I was afraid I might…"

"Afraid of what?"

"It doesn't matter now. It's no longer an issue. We'll consider it bad luck all around that I ended up where I ended up during that storm."

She drew herself in. "Now, I won't embarrass my uncle or the rest of my family by arguing with one of his guests, however insufferable. While you're here, I suggest we do our best to stay out of each other's way." She turned her back on him. "I have nothing more to say to you."

"Some hospitality—Cordinian style."

Shocked to the bone, she whirled back. "My mother—" she nearly choked. "My mother offered you and your family an invitation to our country, to her brother's home. You will receive every courtesy—publicly—from my family and from me. In private…" What hissed through her teeth was an insult more usually heard in a French gutter than a palace garden. Del only raised his eyebrows.

"Nice mouth, Your Highness."

"And now, there is nothing more to be said between us."

"I've got plenty to say to you, sister."

His tone, the term, made sentimental tears want to rise in her throat. Turning her back on him, she did what she could to force them back. "Sir, you are dismissed."

"Oh, stuff a sock in it." Out of patience, he spun her back around. Then froze when he saw the sparkle of tears. "What are you doing? Stop that. If you think you're going to pull out the waterworks to make me feel like a heel, think again."

He took a deliberate step back from her as he searched his pockets. "Look, God. I don't have a handkerchief, so snuffle it back."

"Go away." She was no less appalled than he when a tear spilled over. "Go inside, go back to America, or go to hell. But go away."

"Camilla." Undone, he stepped toward her again.

"Your Highness." Formal in company, and avidly curious, Marian stepped onto the garden path. "I beg your pardon, but Miss Lattimer has arrived. She's been shown to her rooms."

"Sarah?" Surprised, Del stared at Camilla. "You invited Sarah to the palace."

"Yes. I'll be right in, Marian. Thank you. If you'd please show Lord Delaney to his rooms, or anywhere else he'd like to go? Please excuse me, My Lord."

"My Lord?" Marian studied him carefully when Camilla walked quickly away. She was torn between wanting to level him for hurting her dearest friend, and sighing with sympathy over the misery so plain on his face. "May I show you the rest of the gardens?"

"No, thanks. Unless you've got a handy pond or fountain I can soak my head in."

Marian only smiled. "I'm sure we can accommodate you."

He wondered if he'd be doing everyone a favor if he did leave. His mother would be furious, his father baffled. And they would both be embarrassed, but Camilla would, obviously, be relieved.

And he wouldn't have to see her, look at her and try not to remember how she'd looked wearing jeans and a T-shirt while she fried up eggs. Not that she looked anything like that now.

She was polished and sparkling and elegant as the diamonds he'd seen winking at her ears. And just, he tried to convince himself, as cold.

But it occurred to him that he couldn't let her chase him off—the way he'd chased her. He'd stay, if for no other reason than to prove to her what spine was.

It wasn't hard not to get in her way. The palace was a far cry from a five-room cabin in the Vermont woods.

And he couldn't claim not to be enjoying himself, on some level. He liked her brothers, her cousins. It was like watching a pack of handsome, elegant wolves run just short of wild.

As an only child, he'd never been exposed to big, boisterous families. Which, he soon discovered, was what they were under the titles and polish. A family. Closely knit enough that he had trouble remembering who was sibling, who was cousin.

Several of them talked him into going down to the stables—and a hell of a horse palace it was. The minute they discovered he could ride, he was mounted up.

That was how he met Alexander, Cordina's ruler, and his brother, Prince Bennett, Camilla's uncles. And her father, Reeve MacGee.

"Sir." One of the young men—he thought it was Dorian—grinned and made formal introductions.

Del shifted in the saddle. He'd been taught, of course, but months—years—passed without him needing the protocol. He didn't like having to dig it up—and cared less for the sensation of being dissected by three pair of coolly measuring eyes.

"Welcome to Cordina, Lord Brigston," Alex said in a smooth, faintly aloof voice. "And my home."

"Thank you, sir." Del managed what passed for a bow while mounted on a skittish horse.

"We're pleased to have you, and to repay you in some way for the hospitality you showed my niece." There was a subtle and keen edge under the courtesy. Alex made certain of it.

"That horse wants a run," Bennett said because he felt a tug of sympathy. Poor bastard, he thought. Outnumbered. "You look like you can handle him."

Del felt the quick slice of Alex's words—like a nick from a honed fencing sword. He preferred shifting his gaze to the more friendly brother. "He's a beauty."

"We'll let you enjoy your ride. I'd be interested to speak with you regarding your work," Alexander added. "As it's become so much a passion of Princess Camilla's."

"At your convenience, sir."

Alex nodded, then continued to walk his mount toward the stables. After a glance of some pity, Bennett followed behind him. Reeve turned his mount until he was side by side with Del.

"You," he said, pointing at his sons, his nephews. "Take off." Then, turning to Del, he continued, "It's time you and I had a little chat," he said as the echo of hooves faded in the race up the hill. "I'm wondering if you can come up with a good reason why I shouldn't just snap your neck."

Well, Del thought, at least there was no need for protocol and politics now. The man looked like he could give the neck-snapping a good shot. He was fit, broad-shouldered, and his hands appeared to be rough and ready.

And he looked to Del more like a soldier than any farmer he'd ever come across.

"I doubt it," Del decided. "You want to do it here, or somewhere more secluded where you can dump me in a shallow grave?"

Reeve's smile was thin. "Let's take a ride. You make a habit out of taking stray young women into your house, Caine?"

"No. She was the first. I can promise she'll be the last."

The day was warm, but breezy. Del hated the fact that he was sweating. The man had eyes like lasers.

"You want me to believe you took her in out of the goodness of your heart. You had no idea who she was—even though her face is plastered on magazine covers, in newspapers, on television screens all over the world. You had no intention of exploiting her, of using her influence for your own gain. Or of trading off the press with stories about how you took her to bed."

"Just a damn minute." Del reined to a stop, and now it was his gaze that bored heat. "I don't use women. I sure as hell couldn't have used her if I'd tried because she'd have kicked me in the teeth for it. I don't have time for gossip magazines or television, and I wasn't expecting to find some runaway princess stranded on the side of the road in a storm. She said she was low on funds so I gave her a place to stay and a job. I didn't ask her a lot of questions or pay much attention."

"Well, enough attention, apparently, to take her to bed."

"That's right. And that's nobody's business but ours. You want to kick my ass over that, you go ahead. But you start accusing me of taking what we had between us and turning it into some cheap splash for the media, I'm kicking yours right back."

Right answer, Reeve thought. Exactly right. He shifted in the saddle. The boy had guts, he decided, pleased. But that was no reason not to torture him. "What are your intentions toward my daughter?"

The angry flush faded until Del was sheet pale. "My—my— What?"

"You heard the question, son. Roll your tongue back in your mouth and answer it."

"I don't have any. She won't even speak to me. I'm staying out of her way."

"Just when I was beginning to think you weren't a complete jackass after all." Reeve swung his mount around again. "Give that horse a good gallop," he advised. "And don't fall off and break your stiff neck."

As he rode back to the stables, Reeve thought the conversation might not have been precisely what his wife had meant when she'd asked him to have a man-to-man talk with Del. But it had certainly been satisfying.

Camilla would have enjoyed a good gallop herself. But the ladies' tea required her attention and her presence. As the weather was fine, the party was spread over the south terrace and the rose garden so that guests could enjoy the views of the Mediterranean and the fragrance of flowers.

Her aunt had opted for casual elegance so the pretty tables were covered with warm peach cloths and set

with glass dishes of deep cobalt. More flowers, cheer-
ful tropical blooms, spilled out of shallow bowls
while white-coated staff poured flutes of champagne
as well as cups of tea. Each lady was presented with
a silver compact etched with the royal seal.

A harpist plucked strings quietly in the shade of an
arbor tumbled with white roses.

Her aunt Eve, Camilla thought, knew how to set
her stage.

Women in floaty dresses wandered the garden or
gathered in groups. Knowing her duty, Camilla
moved through the guests while she nursed a single
glass of champagne. She smiled, exchanged pleasant-
ries, chatted, and shoved all thoughts of Del into a
corner of her mind, then ruthlessly locked it.

"I've barely had a moment with you." Eve slid an
arm through Camilla's and drew her aside.

She was a small woman with a lovely tumble of
raven hair that provided a exquisite frame for her
diamond-shaped face. Her eyes, a deep and bold blue,
sparkled as she nudged Camilla toward the terrace
wall.

"Not enough time now," she said in a voice that
still carried a hint of her native Texas drawl, "but
later I want to hear about your adventure. Every little
detail."

"Mother's already told you."

"Of course." With a laugh, Eve kissed Camilla's
cheek. Gabriella had done more then tell her—she
had enlisted Eve's help in the matter of prying and
poking. "But that's secondhand information. I like
going to the source."

"I've been waiting for Uncle Alex to call me out
on the carpet."

Eve lifted an eyebrow. "That worries you?"

"I hate upsetting him."

"If I worried about that, I'd spend my life biting my nails." Lips pursed, Eve glanced at her perfect manicure. "Nope. He has to be what he is," she added more soberly, and looked out to the sea that lay blue against the edges of her adopted country. "So much responsibility. He was born for it—and bred for it. As you've been, honey. But he trusts you—completely. And he's very interested in your young man."

"He's not my young man."

"Ah. Well." She remembered, very well, when she'd tried to convince herself Alex, heir to Cordina, wasn't hers. "Let's say he's interested in Lord Delaney's work—and your interest in that work."

"Aunt Chris was a tremendous help," Camilla added, glancing over toward Eve's older sister. She wasn't technically Camilla's aunt, but their family was a very inclusive one.

"Nothing she likes better than a good campaign. That comes from marrying the Gentleman from Texas. The senator was very pleased to discuss the Bardville Research Project with his associates in Florida."

"After Aunt Chris talked him into it, and I'm very grateful to her. She looks wonderful, by the way."

"Like a newlywed," Eve agreed. "After five years of marriage. She always said she was holding out for the perfect man. I'm glad she found him. Whether it takes fifty years or five minutes," she said, giving Camilla's hand a quick squeeze, "when it's right, you know it. And when you know it and you're smart, you don't take no for an answer. Something like that is worth fighting for. Well, back to work."

Camilla stopped by the tables, found a precious three minutes to speak with her young cousin Marissa. She watched her sister, Adrienne, sit and with apparently good cheer, talk with an elderly Italian countess who was deaf as a post.

Hannah, her uncle Bennett's wife, gestured her over to a shady table where she sat enjoying tea and scones with Del's mother.

"Lady Brigston and I have a number of mutual acquaintances," Hannah explained. "I've been badgering her about her work, and now I'm dreaming about running off to dig for dinosaur bones."

There had been a time when, as a British agent, adventure had been Hannah's lifework. But as a princess, and mother of two active sons, she'd traded one kind of adventure for another.

As an agent, she'd had to deliberately downplay her looks and bury her love of fashion, now she could indulge them. Her dark blond hair was sleeked back in a twist. Her sleeveless tea dress showed off athletic arms and was the same vivid green as her eyes.

"I'd like that myself." Smiling, Camilla obeyed Hannah's signal and sat. "Though I imagine it's hard, tedious work. You must love it," she said to Alice.

"It's what I always wanted to do—even as a child. Other girls collected dolls. I collected fossils."

"It's so rewarding," Camilla commented, "to know, always, what you want, and be able to work toward it."

"Indeed." Alice inclined her head. "And tremendously exciting, I'd think, to discover an advocation along the way—and work toward it."

"Oh. Would you excuse me a moment?" Recognizing her cue, Hannah rose. "I need to speak with Mrs. Cartwright." She exchanged a quick and telling look with Alice—and got out of the way.

"Your family, if I may say so, Your Highness, is wonderful."

"Thank you. I agree with you."

"I'm, as a rule, more comfortable in the company of men. Simply don't have much in common with females. So fussy about the oddest things, to my mind."

The hand she waved had nails that were short and unpainted. She wore only a simple gold band on her ring finger. "But I feel very much at home with your mother, your aunts," she went on. "It's no wonder I'm already so fond of you."

"Thank you," Camilla said again, a little flustered. "That's very kind."

"Are you very angry with my son?"

"I—"

"Not that I blame you," Alice went on before Camilla could formulate a diplomatic answer. "He can be such a...what's the word I'm looking for? Oh, yes. Bonehead. Such a bonehead. He gets it from his father, so he really can't help it. He must've given you a terrible time."

"No. Not at all."

"No need to be tactful." She patted Camilla's hand. "It's just we two, and I know my boy in and out. Terrible manners—partially my fault, I can't deny it. I never was one to bother about the niceties. Outrageous temper—that's his father's—always booming around. Forgets why half the time after the explosion—which is annoying and frustrating to the other party. Don't you think?"

"Yes—" With a half laugh, Camilla shook her head. "Lady Brigston, you're putting me in an awkward position. Let me say I admire your son's work—his approach to it and his passion for it. On a personal level, we have what you might call a conflict in styles."

"You have been well raised, haven't you?" Gabriella had warned her it wouldn't be easy to chip through the composure. "Do you mind if I tell you a little story? There was once a young American girl, barely twenty-one with her college degree hot in her hand. She had a fire in her belly, one burning ambition. Paleontology. Most thought her mad," she added with a twinkle. "After all what was a young woman doing fiddling around with dinosaur bones? She wheedled her way onto a dig—this particular dig because the man in charge was someone who's work—his approach to it and his passion for it—she admired."

She paused, smiled and sipped her tea. "She read his books, read articles on or by him. He was, to her, a great hero. Imagine her reaction when he turned out to be this big, irritable, impatient man who barely acknowledged her existence—and then mostly to complain about it."

"He is like his father," Camilla murmured.

"Oh, the spitting image," Alice acknowledged with some pride. "They sniped at each other, this rude man and this brash young woman. She did most of the sniping as he was so thickheaded most of her best shots just bounced off his skull. It was utterly infuriating."

"Yes," Camilla said almost to herself. "Infuriating."

"He was fascinating. So brilliant, so handsome, so—apparently—disinterested in her. Though he began to soften, just a little, toward her as she was damn good at the work and had a sharp, seeking mind. Caine men admire a sharp, seeking mind."

"Apparently."

"She fell madly in love with him, and after getting over being annoyed with herself over that, she put that sharp mind to work. She pursued him, which flustered him. He found all manner of reasons why this shouldn't be. He was fifteen years older, he didn't have time for females and so on. She had a few quibbles herself. This Earl of Brigston business just didn't fit into her Yankee system very well. It might have discouraged her, but she was stubborn—and she knew, in her heart, he had feelings for her. And since the title came with the man, and she wanted the man, she decided she could live with it. So what could she do but seduce him?"

Because Alice looked at Camilla for agreement, Camilla nodded obediently. "Naturally."

"He stammered and stuttered and looked, for a delightful few moments, like a panicked horse caught in a stable fire. But she had her way with him. And three weeks later, they were married. It seems to be working out well," she added with a little smile.

"She was an admirable young woman."

"Yes, she was. And she gave birth to an admirable, if knot-headed son. Do you love him?"

"Lady Brigston—"

"Oh, please, call me Alice. I look at you, and I see a young woman, so bright, so fresh, so unhappy. I

know my place, but I'm looking at Camilla, not Her
Royal Highness.''

"He sees the title, and forgets the woman who
holds it.''

"If you want him, don't let him forget. You put
flowers in his house,'' she said, quietly now. "I never
remember to do that sort of thing myself. You know
he kept them, after you'd gone.''

Tears swam into her eyes. "He just didn't notice
them.''

"Yes. He did. Part of him wants to step away from
you and bury himself in his work again. I imagine
both of you—being strong, capable young people—
will do very well if you go your separate ways. But
I wonder what the two of you might do, might make,
if you break through this barrier of pride and hurt and
come together. Don't you?''

Yes, Camilla thought. Constantly. "I told him I
loved him,'' she murmured, "and he turned me
away.''

With a hiss of breath, Alice sat back. "What an
ass. Well then, I have one piece of advice. Camilla.
Make him crawl a little—it'll be good for him—before he tells you the same. I have no doubt you can
manage it.''

Del suffered through a formal, and to his mind in-
terminable, dinner party. He was seated between the
deaf Italian countess and Camilla's sister, Adrienne.
The single advantage was that Camilla's father was
seated well across the enormous dining room.

It would, he decided, be more difficult for her dad
to stab him with his dinner knife that way.

By the time the main course was served, he'd reversed his initial impression of Adrienne as a vapid if ornamental girl. She was, he realized, simply an incredibly sweet-natured woman who was both blissfully happy and quietly charming.

Her help with the countess saved his sanity. And when Adrienne glanced at him, a quick sparkle in her eyes, he saw some of Camilla's sly humor.

He found himself telling her about some of his work as she asked questions specifically designed to encourage it. It didn't occur to him until later that her talent was in drawing people out.

"No wonder Camilla's so fascinated." Adrienne smiled. She had, he'd noted, her mother's soothing voice and her father's sizzling blue eyes. "She always enjoyed puzzles—and that's your work, really, isn't it? A complex puzzle. I was never very good at them. Will you go back to Florida soon?"

"Yes, very soon." He shouldn't be here at all, he told himself.

"When my children are a bit older, we'll take them there. To Disney World." She looked across the table at her husband.

It was that look he'd think of later as well. The sheer contentment in it. The look that had been missing from Camilla's face, he thought, except for the briefest of times.

It had been there. He remembered it being there, when she'd stretched out on the bank of his pond. *Camilla Content,* he'd called her. And then she'd been gone.

Chapter Eleven

For a princess she worked like a horse. It made it difficult for a man to manage five minutes alone with her to apologize.

Del wasn't sure exactly what he was apologizing for, but he was beginning to think she had one coming.

Guilt—a taste he didn't care for—had been stuck in his throat since he'd seen that tear run down her cheek. Adding to it were various members of her family who were so bloody friendly, or gracious—or both at the same time—he was beginning to feel like a jackass.

Even her mother had cornered him. If that was an acceptable definition of being taken gently aside to be given a warm and graceful expression of her gratitude for opening his home to her daughter.

"I know she's a grown woman," Gabriella said as

she stood with him on a rise overlooking the gem-blue waters of the Mediterranean. "And a capable one. But I'm a mother, and we tend to worry."

"Yes, madam." He agreed, though he'd never considered his mother much of a worrier.

"I worried less when I knew she was with someone trustworthy and kind—who she obviously respected." Gabriella continued to smile, even when he—quite visibly—winced. "I'd been concerned about her for some time."

"Concerned?"

"She'd been working too hard for too long. Since the death of my father, and her own blossoming, you could say, there have been more demands on her time, her energies."

"Your daughter has considerable energy."

"Yes, as a rule. I'm afraid she's been more exposed to the appetites of the media in the last year or two than anyone could be prepared for."

Could he understand? Gabriella wondered. Could anyone who hadn't lived it? She hoped he could.

"She's lovely, as you know, and vibrant—as well as the oldest female of her generation of the family. The media's pursuit of her has been voracious, and I'm afraid it cost her, emotionally. Even physically. I know what it's like. I used to slip away myself. There are times the need to be away, even from something dear to your heart, is overwhelming. Don't you think?"

"Yes. I have Vermont."

Her face went soft, and bright. Yes, she thought, he could understand. "And I had my little farm. Until, I think, very recently, Camilla hadn't found her place to be away. To be quiet, even if it was just inside her mind. Thank you." She rose up and kissed his cheek. "Thank you for helping her find it."

He might have felt lower, Del thought when they parted, if he crawled on his belly and left a slimy trail behind him.

He had to talk to Camilla. Reasonably. Rationally. There were questions now, and he wanted them answered. It seemed only right a man should have some answers before he did that crawling.

But every time he made some subtle inquiry about her, he was told she was in a meeting, taking an appointment, engaged with her personal assistant.

He wanted to think all this meant manicures or shopping or whatnot, until Adrienne corrected him. "I'm sorry, were you looking for Camilla?"

"No." It felt awkward lying to that soft, pretty smile. "Not exactly, madam. I haven't seen her this morning."

Adrienne cuddled her baby daughter. "She's doing double duty, I'm afraid. My oldest isn't feeling quite well, and I don't like to leave him. She's filling in for me at the hospital. I was scheduled to visit the pediatric ward, but with little Armand so fussy, I wanted to be close."

"Ah...I hope he's all right."

"He's napping now, and seems much better. I thought I'd bring the baby out for some sunshine before I went back up to check on him. But Camilla should be back in an hour. No," she corrected. "She has an appointment with Mama regarding the Art Center afterward. I know she normally deals with correspondence midafternoon, though where she'll find the time today is beyond me."

She kept the soft smile on her face and the delighted laughter inside. The poor man, she thought, was so frustrated. And so in love with her sister.

"Is there something I can do for you?"

"No. No, madam, thank you."

"I believe Dorian escaped down to the stables," she said kindly. "Several of the guests are making use of the horses, if you'd like to join them."

He didn't, but wished he had when he was summoned by Prince Alexander.

"Lord Brigston, I hope you haven't been neglected since your arrival."

"Not at all, Your Highness."

The office reflected the man, Del thought. Both were elegant, male and polished by tradition. The prince exuded power along with dignity. His hair was black as night and threaded with silver. His aristocratic face was honed to sharp angles. Dark, his eyes were equally sharp and very direct.

"Since the Princess Camilla has expressed such a keen interest, I've studied some of your work. My family's interests," he said in a tone smooth as a polished dagger, "are mine. Tell me more about this current project of yours."

Though he resented being made to feel like a student auditioning, Del obliged. He understood perfectly, and knew he was meant to understand, that he was being measured and judged.

When, in twenty minutes, he was graciously dismissed, Del wasn't certain if he'd passed the audition or if he should keep a wary eye out for the executioner.

But he did know the back of his neck prickled as the image of an ax poised above it hovered in his mind.

Any man, he decided, who considered—however remotely considered—becoming involved with a member of the royal family of Cordina needed his head examined. While it was still safely on his shoulders.

Del had always considered himself perfectly sane.

To stay that way, he decided to escape for a couple of hours. It wasn't a simple matter. A man couldn't just call a damn cab to come pick him up at the palace. There was procedure, protocol, policy. In the end, Camilla's older brother Kristian casually offered him the use of a car—and a driver if he liked.

Del took the car and skipped the driver.

And came as close to falling in love with a place not his own as he'd ever in his life.

There was something stunning about it—the tiny country on the sea. It made him think of jewels—old and precious ones passed down from generation to generation.

The land rose in tiers of hills from the lap of the sea. Houses, pink and white and dull gold tumbled up and down those rises, jutted out on the promontory, as if they'd been carved there. Flowers—he'd been paying more attention to them since Camilla—grew in abundance and with such a free and casual air they added immense charm to the drama of rock and cliff. The fronds of regal palms fluttered in a constant balmy breeze.

The sense of age appealed to him. Generation by generation, century by century, this small gem had survived and gleamed, and clung to its heart without giving way to the frenzied rush of urbanity, without exploiting its vast and staggering views with skyscrapers.

He imagined it had changed here and there over time. No place remained the same, and that was the beauty of man. And when man had wisdom along with invention, he managed to find a way to preserve the heart while feeding the mind.

The Bissets, who had ruled here for four centuries, had obviously been wise.

He stopped on the drive back, along the winding, rising road, to study the place of princes. It was only just, he supposed, that the palace stood on the highest point. It faced the sea, its white stones rising from the cliff. It spread, even rambled with its battlements, its parapets and towers harking proudly back to another age. Another time.

Wars, he thought, and royalty. Historic bedfellows.

Even in modern times a small, ugly little war had been fought here. When he'd been a boy a self-styled terrorist had attempted to assassinate members of the royal family. Camilla's mother had been kidnapped. Her aunt, then simply Eve Hamilton, had been shot.

He realized now that he hadn't considered that, or how such a history so close to the heart could and did affect Camilla.

Still, she hadn't let it stop her from striking out on her own, alone, he thought now. It didn't stop her from coming back here, to the castle on the hill, and taking up her family duties.

The country, the family, was at peace now. But peace was a fragile thing.

He imagined those who lived inside understood the palace had been built for defense. And his archaeologist's eye could see how cagey the design. There could be no attack from the sea, no force that could breech the sheer rock walls of the cliffs. And the height, the hills made it all but impregnable.

Its port made it rich.

It had also been built for beauty. He considered the quest for beauty a very human need.

Standing where he was, he wouldn't have thought of it as a home, but only as a symbol. But he had been inside, beyond those iron gates. However powerful, or symbolic, or aesthetically potent, it was a home.

Perhaps she lived a part of her life on a farm in Virginia, but this place, this palace, this country, was very much her home.

It had to be obvious to both of them that it couldn't be his.

When he drove back through the gates, passed the bold red uniforms of the palace guards, a cloud of depression came with him.

"He's in a horrible mood," Alice confided to Gabriella when they stole five minutes in the music room. They huddled close, as conspirators should. "Apparently he went out for a drive and came back brooding and snarly. It's a good sign."

"Camilla's been distracted and out of sorts all afternoon. It's going perfectly. Oh, and my spies tell me Delaney asked about her several times this morning."

"The best thing was her being so busy and unavailable. Give that boy time to think."

"He won't be able to think when he sees her tonight. Oh, Alice, she looks so beautiful in her gown. I was at her last fitting, and she's just spectacular."

"They're going to make us beautiful grandchildren," Alice said with a sigh.

He didn't like wearing black tie. There were so many pieces to it, why a man needed all those pieces where a shirt and pants did the job was beyond him.

But he'd made up his mind to leave in the morning, so that was something. He'd already come up with the necessary excuse for his early departure—an urgent e-mail from the site.

No one would know the difference.

He'd fulfill his obligation tonight—for his parents—find a way to apologize or at least come to terms with Camilla. And then get back to reality as soon as possible. He wasn't a man for palaces. Digging under one maybe—now that could be interesting.

All he had to do was survive the sticky formality of one more evening. He was sure he could manage to slip out early from that event as well. In the morning, he'd pay his respects to his hosts, then get the hell out of Dodge.

Only one little chore had to be done first. He had to—in all good conscience—express his appreciation for the help in funding to Camilla. Face-to-face, and without the stiffness he'd fallen back on in correspondence.

That had been small of him and unworthy of her gesture.

Dressed, and wanting nothing more than to get the entire ordeal over with, he joined his parents in their sitting room.

"Well, hell, look at you." It was a rare event to see his mother elegantly attired. He grinned, circling his finger so that she turned. The simple black gown showed off her trim, athletic figure, and the Brigston pearls added panache.

"You're a babe," he decided and made her laugh.

"I figure I can stand these shoes for about an hour and a half, after that, it's anybody's guess." She walked over to straighten her husband's formal tie.

"Don't fuss, Alice. I'm getting rid of the damn thing at the first opportunity." Still Niles smiled as he leaned down to kiss her cheek. "But the boy's right. You are a babe."

"This 'do' will be crawling with babes. Speaking of which," Alice said casually to her son, "have you seen Camilla today?"

"No."

"Ah, well. You'll see her tonight."

"Right." With hundreds of people around, he thought. How the hell would he manage to say what he had to say—once he figured out what that was—when they were surrounded? "Let's get this over with," Del suggested.

"God. Just like your father." Resigned, Alice took each of her men by the arm.

Guests were formally announced, then escorted to the receiving line. The bows and curtsies went on endlessly in Del's estimation. Then he got his first look at Camilla, and forgot everything else.

She wore a gown the same tawny gold as her eyes. In it, she was iridescent. Luminous. It left her shoulders bare, nipped in to a tiny waist, then simply flowed out with what seemed like miles of skirt that shimmered like sun-drenched water in the elegant light of countless chandeliers.

White and yellow diamonds sparkled at her ears, dripped in complex tiers toward the swell of her breast. And fired in the tiara set on the glossy cap of her hair.

She was, in that moment, the embodiment of the fairy-tale princess. Beauty, grace and elegance, and all of them bone-deep.

He had never felt so much the frog.

But he thought—hoped—he'd managed to roll his eyes back into his head by the time he reached her.

"My Lord."

"Madam." He took the hand she offered, sliding his thumb over her knuckles. Had this woman actually scrambled eggs for him? If this was reality, maybe all the rest had been some complex fantasy.

"I hope you'll enjoy your evening."

"I wasn't planning on it."

Her polite smile never wavered. "Then I hope you don't find it overly tedious."

"I need five minutes," he murmured.

"I'm afraid this is an inconvenient time. Let go of my hand," she said in an undertone as his grip tightened. "People are watching."

"Five minutes," he said again and their eyes locked, then he reluctantly moved up the line.

Her heart might have raced, but she continued to stand, smile and greet guests. The combination of willpower and breeding stopped her from giving into the towering urge to crane her neck and find Del in the crowd moving into the ballroom. Curiosity pierced with a splinter of hope made her almost ill by the time her aunt and uncle opened Cordina's Autumn Ball.

He'd looked at her—hadn't he—as he had at odd

moments in the cabin. As if she were the center of his thoughts.

But, as she and her cousin Luc crossed the floor for their first dance, she had no time for private thoughts.

When the palace opened its doors for a ball, it opened them wide and with brilliant ceremony. Glamour was allowed full sway here and given the satin edge of pomp. Waterfalls of chandeliers showered light on dazzling gowns, glittering jewels, banks of sumptuous flowers. Frothy champagne bubbled in crystal.

On the terrace beyond there was the seductive glow of candles and torchères. Hundreds of antique mirrors lined the walls and threw back reflection after reflection of gorgeously gowned women and elegantly garbed men as they spun around the polished floor.

Jewels flashed, and music soared.

Camilla danced, for duty and for pleasure, and then for love with her father.

"I watched you and Mama."

"Watched us what?"

"Dancing just a bit ago. And I thought, look at them." She pressed her cheek to his. "How can anyone look anywhere but at them. They're so beautiful."

"Did I ever tell you about the first time I saw her?"

Camilla leaned back to laugh into his eyes. "A million times. Tell me again."

"It was her sixteenth birthday. A ball, very much like this. She wore a pale green dress, not so different from what you're wearing now. All those billowing skirts that make a woman look like a fantasy. Diamonds in her hair, the way they're in yours tonight.

I fell in love with her on the spot, though I didn't see her again for ten years. She was the most exquisite thing I'd ever laid eyes on.''

He looked down at her daughter. "Now I'm dancing with the second most exquisite thing."

"Daddy." She took her hand from his shoulder to touch his face. "I love you so much. I'm sorry you were mad at me."

"I wasn't mad, baby. Worried, but not mad. Now as far as that jackass you were with—"

"Daddy."

The warning light in her eye had him glaring right back at her. "I have one thing to say about him. He has potential."

"You don't really know—" She broke off, narrowed her eyes suspiciously. "Is this a trap?"

"I used to worry that some slick-talking pretty boy was going to come along and sweep you off before you realized he was a jerk. Well, you certainly can't call Caine slick-talking or pretty."

"No, indeed."

"And since you already know he's a jerk, you're in good shape," he added, making her laugh. "I want you happy, Cam. Even more than I want to keep my little girl all to myself."

"You're going to make me cry."

"No, you won't cry." He drew her close again. "You're made of sterner stuff than that."

"I love him, Daddy."

"I know." Reeve's eyes met Del's across the crowds of dancers. "Poor son of a bitch doesn't have a prayer. You go get him, honey. And if he doesn't come around quick enough, let me know. I'd still like a reason to kick his ass."

* * *

"Make up your mind, Delaney."

"About what?"

Alice took the wine she'd asked him to fetch. "Whether you're just going to scowl at Camilla half the night, or ask her to dance."

"She hasn't stopped dancing for two minutes all night, has she?"

"It's part of her job. Or do you think she likes dancing with that pizza-faced young man with the buck teeth who's stepping all over her feet? Go. Dance with her."

"If you think I'm lining up with half the men in this place—"

"I'd say you'd lost your wits," Alice finished. "Go, cut in. Another minute with that clumsy boy and she'll have a permanent limp."

"All right, all right." Put that way, it was like doing her a favor. Sort of like riding to the rescue, he decided as he saw—quite clearly—the wince flicker over her face as her feet were stomped on again.

Feeling more heroic with each step, Del threaded through the dancers. He tapped Camilla's partner on the shoulder, and moved in so smoothly he surprised himself.

"Cutting in." He whirled Camilla away before the boy could do more than gawk and stammer.

"That was rude."

"Did the trick. How're your feet?"

Her lips twitched. "Other than a few broken toes, holding up, thank you. You dance quite well, My Lord."

"Been a while, but it comes back to you, Madam.

Either way, I couldn't be worse than your last partner. Figured you needed a break.''

''Rescuing the damsel in distress?'' She arched her eyebrows. ''Really, twice in one lifetime. Be careful or you'll make it a habit. You said you needed five minutes with me—and that was nearly two hours ago. Did you change your mind?''

''No.'' But he was no longer clear on what to do with five minutes. Not now that he was holding her again. ''I wanted to… About the project. The funding.''

''Ah.'' Disappointment sank into her belly. ''If it's business, I'll see that Marian schedules an appointment for you tomorrow.''

''Camilla. I wanted to thank you.''

She softened, just a little. ''You're welcome. The project's important to me, too, you know.''

''I guess I get that. Now.'' He had only to angle his head, dip it a little, and his mouth could be on hers. He wanted, more than anything, to have one long taste of her again. Even if it was the last time. ''Camilla—''

''The dance is finished.'' But her gaze stayed locked with his, and her voice was thick. ''You have to let me go.''

He knew that. He knew exactly that. But not quite yet. ''I need to talk to you.''

''Not here. For heaven's sake, if you don't let me go you'll have your name splashed all over the papers tomorrow.'' She smiled, gaily.

''I don't give a damn.''

''You haven't lived with it all your life, as I have. Please, step back. If you want to talk, we'll go out on the terrace.''

When he relaxed his grip, she eased away, then spoke clearly and in the friendliest of tones for all the pricked ears nearby. "It's warm. I wonder, Lord Delaney, if you'd join me for some fresh air? And I'd love a glass of champagne."

"No problem."

She slid an arm through his as they walked off the dance floor. "My brothers tell me you ride very well. I hope you'll continue to enjoy the stables while you're here." She kept up the casual chatter as he lifted a flute of champagne from a silver tray and offered it.

"Do you ride, Madam?"

"Certainly." She sipped, strolled toward the open terrace doors. "My father breeds horses on his farm. I've ridden all my life."

A number of other guests had spilled out onto the terrace. Before Camilla could walk to the rail, Del simply tugged her arm, the wine sloshing to the rim of her glass as he steered her briskly toward the wide stone steps.

"Slow down." She paused at the top. "I can't jog down stairs in this dress. I'll break my neck."

He took her glass from her, then stood restlessly by as she gracefully lifted her billowing skirts with her free hand. At the base of the steps, he set the champagne—barely touched—on the closest table, then continued to pull her down one of the garden paths.

"Stop dragging me along," she hissed. "People will—"

"Oh, lighten up," he snapped.

She grit her teeth as she struggled to maintain her dignity. "See how light you are when gossipmongers in ten countries are tossing your name around tomorrow. In any case, I'm wearing three-inch heels and five miles of skirt. Just slow down.''

"I don't listen to gossip, so I won't hear them tossing my name around. And if I slow down too long, somebody's going to jump out of some corner with something for you to do. Or to fawn and scrape. Or just say something so they can say they've spoken to you. I want five damn minutes alone with you.''

The retort that rose to her lips faded away.

Sparkling silver luminaries lighted a path that was already streamed with moonlight. She could smell the romance of night jasmine and roses, hear it in the pulse and pound of the sea. And her own heart.

Her lover wanted to be alone with her.

He didn't stop until the music was barely more than a murmur in the distance. "Camilla.''

She held her breath. "Delaney.''

"I wanted to—'' She wore moonlight like pearls, he thought, too dazzled to be astonished by the poetic turn of mind. Her skin was sheened with it. Her eyes glowed. The diamonds in her hair sparked, reminding him there was heat inside the elegance.

He tried again. "I wanted to apologize for... To tell you—''

She didn't know who moved first. It didn't seem to matter. All that mattered was they were in each other's arms. Their mouths met, once, twice. Frantically. Then a third time, long and deep.

"I missed you.'' He pulled her closer, rocking when she was locked against him. "God, I missed you.''

The words seemed to pour into her. "Don't let go. Don't let me go.''

"I didn't think I'd ever see you again." He turned his head to race kisses over her face. "I didn't mean to ever see you again."

"I wasn't ever going to see you again first," she said with a laugh. "Oh, I was so angry when I got that letter. That stiff, formal, nasty letter: 'We of the Bardville Research Project wish to express our sincere appreciation.' I could've murdered you."

"You should've seen the first draft." He eased back enough to grin at her. "It was a lot…pithier."

"I'd probably have preferred it." She threw her arms around his neck. "Oh, I'm so happy. I've been trying to figure out how to live without you. Now I won't have to. After we're married, you can teach me how to read one of those lab reports with all those symbols. I never could…"

She trailed off because he'd gone so completely still. Her soaring heart fell back to earth with a rude and painful thud. "You don't love me." Her voice was quiet, scrupulously calm as she eased out of his arms. "You don't want to marry me."

"Let's just slow down, okay? Marriage—" His throat closed up on the word. "Let's be sensible, Camilla."

"Of course. All right, let's." Now her tone was terrifyingly pleasant. "Why don't you go first?"

"There are… There are issues here," he began, frantically trying to clear his jumbled brain long enough to think.

"Very well." She folded her hands. "Issue number one?"

"Cut that out. You just cut that out." He paced down the path, back again. "I have a very demanding, time-consuming profession."

"Yes."

"When I'm in the field, I usually live in a trailer that makes the cabin look like a five-star hotel."

"Yes?"

He bared his teeth, but snagged his temper back at the last minute. "You can't stand there, with that palace at your back while you're wearing a damn crown and tell me you don't see there's a problem."

"So, issue one is our different lifestyles and separate responsibilities."

"In a nutshell. And neatly glossing over the tiaras and glass slippers. Yeah."

"Glass slippers?" That snapped it. "Is that how you see me, and my life—as one ball after the next, one magic pumpkin ride? I have just as vital a role in the world in my glass slippers as you do in your work boots."

"I'm not saying you don't. That's the whole point." He tugged his formal tie loose and dragged it off. "This isn't what I do. I can't strap myself up like a penguin every time I turn around because you have a social obligation. But you should have someone who would. And I'm not asking you to chuck your diamonds to live in camp in the middle of nowhere. It's ridiculous. It would never work."

"That's where you're wrong. My father was a cop who wanted to farm. Who wanted, more than anything, peace and quiet and to work on the land. My mother was—is—a princess. When they met she was the chatelaine of this place. She had taken up the responsibility as hostess, as ambassador, as symbolic female head of this country when her mother died. But you see, they loved each other so they found a way to give to each other what they needed, to accept the responsibilities and obligations each brought with them, and to make a life together.''

Her chin was up now, her eyes glittering. ''They make me proud. And I'm determined to be every bit the woman my mother is. But you, you with your excuses and your pitiful issues, you're not half the man my father is. *He* had courage and spine and romance. He isn't intimidated by a crown because he respects and understands the woman who wears it.''

She swept up her skirts again. ''I would have lived in your trailer and still have been a princess. My duty to my name—and yours—would never be shirked. It's you who doubt you could live in this palace and still be a man.''

Chapter Twelve

He hated one single fact the most. She was right. Under all the issues and trappings and complications, he'd been...well, he didn't like the term intimidated. Leery, he decided as he stalked around the gardens as he was wont to stalk around his forest in Vermont. He was leery of linking himself with the princess.

He'd been paying attention in the weeks they'd been apart. He'd seen her face and name splashed over the media. He'd read the stories about her personal life, the speculations about her romantic liaisons.

He knew damn well she wasn't and hadn't been having some hot affair with a French actor as all the articles had trumpeted. She'd been too busy having one with a half-American archaeologist.

Besides, anyone who knew her could see the actor wasn't her type. Too smooth for Camilla.

And that was part of it. The stories, the innuendoes, the outright fabrications were, for the most part, written by people who didn't know her. Who didn't understand how hard she was willing to work, or her devotion to her mother's country. Her great love of her family, and theirs for her.

They saw an image. The same one he'd let himself be blinded by.

But damn it all to hell and back, the woman had leaped from possible, tentative relationship into marriage so quickly it had been like a sucker punch to the jaw. She didn't give a guy a chance to test his footing.

All or nothing with her, he thought darkly as he jammed his hands into his pockets and reviewed the situation.

First, he finally figures out he's in love with her, then he gets poked in the eye with the fact she's been lying to him. Before he can clear his vision on that, she's long gone. So what that he'd told her to go.

Now, after he'd realized the whole situation was totally impossible, she had to stand there looking like something out of a dream and make him see just how much he'd be losing. And just when he'd started to think maybe, maybe, with time and effort, they could get back what they'd had, she kicked him square in the teeth with marriage.

Yeah, give her a month in a trailer in Florida, toss in a few tropical storms, knee-deep mud, bugs the size of baseballs, and...

She'd be great. He stopped dead in his tracks. She'd be fantastic. She was the kind of woman you could plunk down anywhere, in any situation and she'd find a way. She just kept hacking and prodding and fiddling until she found the way.

Because that was Camilla.

He'd fallen for that, he realized. Before he'd fallen for the looks, the style, the heat, he'd lost his head over her sheer determination to find the answers.

And he was letting a minor detail like royal blood stand in his way.

He wanted the woman, and the princess came along with her. Not half the man her father was? Oh, she'd tried to slice him up with that one. He didn't have courage, backbone. He had no romance?

He'd give her some romance that would knock her out of her glass slippers.

He turned, stormed halfway back to the ballroom before he stopped himself. That, he realized, was just the sort of thing he was going to have to avoid. If this relationship was going to have a chance in hell of working he was going to have to think ahead. A man went charging into a palace ball, tossed a princess over his shoulder and started carting her off, he was going to get them both exactly the sort of press she hated.

And likely end up tossed in some dark, damp dungeon for his trouble.

What a man had to do was work out a clear, rational plan—and carry it out where there were no witnesses.

So he sat down on a marble bench and began to do precisely that.

He got rope at the stables. There were times, he was forced to admit, where being a viscount came in handy. Stable hands were too polite to question the eccentricities of Lord Delaney.

He had to wait until the last waltz was over, and guests were tucked in to bed or were on the other side of the palace gates. That only gave him more time to work out logistics—and to wonder what his parents would do if he ended up breaking his idiotic neck.

He knew where her room was now. That had been a simple matter of subtly pumping Adrienne. He could only be grateful her windows overlooked the gardens where there were plenty of shadows. Though he doubted any guards who patrolled the area would be looking for a man dangling several stories up by a rope.

Even when that man swore bitterly when he swung, nearly face first, into those white stone walls. Rapelling down from the parapet had seemed a lot easier in theory than in fact. He was fairly proficient at it from his work, but climbing down a building at night was considerably different. The cold reality had him swinging in the wind with scraped knuckles and strained temper.

He didn't mind the height so much, unless he thought about the possibility of it being his last view. And all, he mused as he tried for a foothold on a stone balcony rail, because she'd pinched at his ego.

Just couldn't wait until morning. Oh, no, he thought as his foot skidded and he went swinging again. That would've been too easy, too ordinary. Too sane. Why have a civilized conversation in broad daylight and tell a woman you love her and want to marry her when you can do something really *stupid* like commit suicide on the bricks below her bedroom window?

That made a statement.

He managed to settle his weight on the rail, and catch his breath. And the rising wind swept in a brisk September rain.

"Perfect." He glanced up to the heavens. "That just caps it."

While the sudden downpour had rain streaming into his eyes, he swung out again, kicked lightly off the wall, and worked his way down to Camilla's private terrace.

The first bolt of lightning crashed over the sea as he dropped down, thankfully, to solid stone. He fought with the knot of the thoroughly wet rope he'd looped around. It took him two drenching minutes to free himself. Dumping the rope, he pushed his sopping hair out of his eyes and marched to her terrace doors.

Found them locked.

For a moment he only stood, staring at them. What the hell did she lock the balcony doors for? he wondered with rising irritation. She was three stories up, in a damn palace with guards everywhere.

How often did she have some idiot climb down the wall and drop on her terrace?

She'd drawn the curtains, too, so he couldn't see a bloody thing. He considered, with a spurt of cheerfulness, the satisfaction of kicking in the doors.

There was a certain style to that, he thought. A certain panache. However, that would likely be squashed when alarms started to scream.

Here he was, wet as a drowned rat, on her terrace. And the only way to get in was to knock.

It was mortifying.

So he didn't knock so much as hammer.

* * *

Inside, Camilla was using a book as an excuse not to sleep. Every fifteen minutes or so, she actually read a sentence. For the most part, one single fact played over and over in her head.

She'd handled everything badly.

There was no way around it. When she stepped back to look at the big picture, Del had reacted exactly as she'd expect him to react. She had leaped, heart first, into an assumption of marriage.

She'd have been insulted if he'd been the one doing the assuming.

Did love make everyone stupid and careless, or was it just her?

She sighed, turned a page in the book without particular interest. She'd bungled everything, she decided, right from the beginning. Oh, he'd helped. He was such a…what had his mother said? Bonehead. Yes, he was such a bonehead—but she *loved* that about him.

But the blame was squarely on her head.

She hadn't been honest with him, and her reasons for holding back now seemed weak and selfish. His anger, and yes, his hurt, had so shattered her that she'd turned tail and run rather than standing her ground.

Then he'd come to her. Was she so steeped in her own self-pity that she refused to acknowledge that no matter how much pressure had been put on him, he'd never have traveled to Cordina unless he'd wanted to see her?

Even tonight he'd taken a step. Instead of taking one in return, she'd recklessly leaped. She'd taken for granted that he'd simply fall in line. Obviously she was too used to people doing so. Wasn't that one of the reasons she'd taken a holiday from being the princess? Had she learned nothing from those weeks as just plain Camilla?

It wasn't just marriage that had caused him to balk. It was the package that came with it. She closed her eyes. She could do nothing about that—would do nothing even if she could. Her family, her blood, her heritage were essential parts of her.

And yet, she wouldn't want a man who shrugged off the complexities of her life. She couldn't love a man who enjoyed the fact that they'd be hounded by the press.

So where did that leave her? Alone, she thought, looking around her lovely, lonely room. Because she'd pushed away the only man she loved, the only man she wanted, by demanding too much, too fast.

No. She slammed the book shut. She wouldn't accept that. Accepting defeat was what had sent her running from the cabin. She wasn't going to do that again. There *had* to be an answer. There had to be a compromise. She would…no. She took a deep breath. *They* would find it.

She tossed the covers aside. She'd go to his room now, she decided. She'd apologize for the things she'd said to him and tell him…*ask* him if there was a way they could start again.

Before she could leap out of bed, the pounding on her terrace doors had her jumping back with her heart in her throat. She grabbed the Georgian silver candlestick from her nightstand as a weapon, and was on the point of snatching up the phone to call security.

"Open the damn door."

She heard the voice boom out, followed by a vicious crack of thunder. Astonished, still gripping her makeshift weapon, she crossed to the doors, and nudged the curtains aside.

She saw him in a flash of lightning. The furious face, the dripping hair, the sopping tuxedo shirt. For a moment she could do nothing but stare with her mouth open.

"Open the damn door," he repeated loudly. "Or I kick it in."

Too stunned to do otherwise, she fumbled with latch and lock. Then she staggered back three steps when he pushed the doors open.

"What?" She could do no more than croak it out as he stood, glaring at her and dripping on the priceless rug.

"You want romance, sister." He grabbed the candle-stick out of her numb fingers and tossed it aside. It looked a little too heavy to risk any accidents, and he had enough bruises for one night.

"Del." She backed up another two steps as he stepped forward. "Delaney. How did you...your hand's bleeding."

"You want backbone? You want adventure? Maybe a little insanity thrown in?" He grabbed her shoulders, lifted her straight to her toes. "How's this?"

"You're all wet," was all she could say.

"You try climbing down the side of a castle in a rainstorm, see what shape you end up in."

"Climb?" She barely registered being pushed across the room. "You climbed down the wall? Have you lost your mind?"

"Damn right. And you know what the guy gets when he breaches the castle walls? He gets the princess."

"You can't just—"

But he could. She discovered very quickly that he could. Before she could clear sheer shock from her system, his mouth was hot on hers. And shock didn't have a chance against need. A thrill swept through her as he dragged her—oh my—to the bed.

He was wet and bleeding and in a towering temper. And he was all hers. She locked her arms around his neck, slid her fingers into that wonderful and dripping hair, and gladly offered him the spoils of war.

Her mouth moved under his, answering his violent kiss with all the joy, all the longing that raged inside her.

The storm burst through the open doors as she released him long enough to tug at his sodden shirt. It landed, somewhere, with a wet plop.

He was surprised his clothes didn't simply steam off him. The heat of his temper paled with the fire that she brought to his blood. So soft, so fragrant, so wonderfully willing. Her face was wet now with the rain he'd brought in with him. He could've lapped it—and her—up like cream.

Undone, he buried his face against her throat. "I need you, damn it. I can't get past it."

"Then have me." Her breath hitched as his hands roamed over her. "Take me."

He lifted his head, looked down at her. Her eyes were dark now, tawny as a cat's. And as her hands came up to frame his face, she smiled. "I've waited so long for you," she murmured. "And I didn't even know."

To prove it, she drew his mouth down to hers again.

Everything he felt for her, about her, from her,

bloomed in the kiss. She trembled from it, and the quiet hum in her throat had his pulse bounding.

That long, white throat fascinated him. The strong slope of her shoulders was a wonder. Damp with rain now, the thin night slip she wore clung provocatively to her body. He took his mouth, his hands over the wet silk first, then the hot, damp flesh beneath.

She moved under him. A graceful arch, a quick shiver. Slowly first, savoring first, he explored, exploited. Excited. When her breathing was thick, her eyes dreamily closed, he dragged her to her knees and ravaged.

He'd catapulted her from quiet pleasure to reckless demand so that she floundered. Drowned in him. Those hard hands that had been so blissfully gentle were now erotically rough. Bowing back, she surrendered to that hungry mouth. Moaned his name as he tore reason to shreds.

She went wild in his arms. As her need pitched to meet his, she tore and tugged at his clothes. Kneeling on the bed, they clung, flesh to flesh, heart raging against heart.

Once more, in a flash of lightning, their eyes met. Held. In his, at last, she saw all she needed to see. And it was she who shifted, taking him in. Wrapping her legs around him to take him deep until they both trembled.

"Je t'aime." She said it clearly though her body quaked. "I love you. I can't help myself."

Before he could speak, her mouth covered his. What was left of his control snapped, whipping his body toward frenzy. She met him, beat for frantic beat. When she closed around him, he swallowed her cry of release. And emptied himself.

"Camilla." He couldn't think past her name, even as he slid down her body to nestle between her breasts. He felt her fingers stroke through his hair and wanted nothing more than to close his eyes and stay steeped in her for the rest of his life.

But his gaze skimmed toward the terrace—and the rain cheerfully blowing in the open doors and soaking floor and rug.

"I didn't close the doors. We're starting to flood. Just stay."

As he rolled away, she watched him lazily. Then she bolted up as he started to cross the room. "No! Wait." She scrambled out of bed, snatched the robe that had been draped over the curved back of her settee. "Someone might see," she muttered, then, with her robe modestly closed, hurried to close the doors herself.

Control, he thought as he watched her draw the drapes. Even now. A princess couldn't walk around naked in front of the windows—not even her own. And certainly couldn't have a man do so.

She turned, saw him eyeing her speculatively. "The guards. Guests," she began, then dropped her gaze. "I'll get some towels."

While she walked into the adjoining bath, he untangled his damp tuxedo pants. They were ruined, he decided, and would be miserably uncomfortable. But if they were going to have a conversation, he wanted to be wearing something besides his heart on his sleeve.

She came back, got down on her hands and knees and began mopping the floor. It made him smile. Made him remember her in his cabin.

"I have to be practical, Delaney."

His brows drew together at the strained edge in her voice. "I understand that."

"Do you?" She hated herself for wanting to weep now.

"Yes, I do. I admire the way you manage to be practical, self-sufficient—and royal."

Her head came up slowly. She eased back to sit on her heels, and the look of surprise on her face was enough to have him shoving his hands in his wet pockets. "I admire you," he said again. "I'm not good with words, these kinds of words. Damn it, do you think I'm an idiot? That I don't have a clue what kind of juggling act you—your whole family—has to perform to be who you are and manage to have any sort of life along with it?"

"No." Looking away from him again, she folded the damp portion of the rug back, then dried the floor beneath it. "No, I believe you understand—as much as you can. Maybe more than another man might. I think that's why, in some ways, we're at odds."

"Why don't you look at me when you talk to me?"

Struggling for composure, she pressed her lips together. But her gaze was level when she lifted her head again. "It's difficult for me. Excuse me a moment." She rose, and shoulders straight as a soldier's, carried the damp towels back to the bath.

Women, Del thought, were a hell of a lot of work.

She came back, went to a small cabinet and took out a decanter. "I think some brandy would help. I was wrong," she began as she poured two snifters. "Tonight in the garden, I was wrong to say those things to you. I apologize."

"Oh, shut up." Out of patience, he snatched a snifter out of her hand.

"Can't you at least pretend to be gracious?"

"Not when you're being stupid. If I want an apology, you'll know it." She'd beat him to the damn apology. Wasn't it just like her? He paced away and though he didn't care for it, took a slug of the brandy. "When you're wrong, I'll let you know it."

He spun back, temper alive on his face. "You hurt me." It infuriated him to admit it.

"I know. The things I said——"

"Not that. That just pissed me off." He dragged a hand through his hair. "You lied to me, Camilla. Or the next thing to it. I started counting on you. And I don't mean to clean up after me. I started thinking about you—about us—a certain way. Then it all blew up in my face."

"I handled it badly. It was selfish—I was selfish," she corrected. "I wanted some time—then more time—to just be. I ran. I told myself it wasn't running away, but it was. Last summer, it was all suddenly too heavy, too close. I couldn't..."

"Just be?"

"I couldn't just be," she said, quietly. "Last summer there was an incident with the press. Not much more, really, no less than so many others the past few years. But it had been building up inside me, all of it until it just got to be too much. I couldn't eat. I wasn't sleeping well, I couldn't concentrate on what I was meant to do. I..."

"No, don't stop. Tell me."

"This incident," she said carefully, "wasn't so different from others. But while it was happening I could hear myself screaming. Inside. I thought—I knew—that unless I got away for a while, the next time it happened, the screams wouldn't be just inside. I was afraid I was having some sort of breakdown.''

"Camilla, for God's sake."

"I should've spoken with my family." She looked back at him because she'd heard that unspoken question in his shocked tone. "They would have understood, supported me, given me time and room. But I just couldn't bring myself to confess such a weakness. Poor Camilla, who's been given every privilege in life, and more—so much more—the unquestioning love from family, is suddenly too delicate, too fragile to deal with the responsibilities and difficulties of her rank and position.''

"That's malarkey."

The term made her laugh a little. And steadied her. "It didn't feel like it at the time. It felt desperate. I was losing myself. I don't know if you can understand that because you know yourself so intimately. But I felt hounded and hunted, and at the same time so unsteady about who I was, inside. What I wanted to do with my life beyond what I was supposed to do, beyond duty. I had no passion for anything, and there's a horrible kind of emptiness to that."

He could imagine it—the pressures, the demands—and the nerves of steel it took to be who she was. The courage, he thought, it had taken to break from all that to find the woman inside.

"So you took off, with a couple suitcases in a rental car, to find it?''

"More or less. And I did find it, though as I said, in the end, I handled it badly.''

"We handled it badly," he corrected. "I was over my head with you, and that was when I thought you were a weird rich chick in some kind of trouble.

When I found out, I figured you'd used me for some kind of a lark.''

She paled. ''It was never—''

''I know that now. I know it. I had feelings for you I've never had for anyone else. I'd worked myself up to tell you—and came into the kitchen and heard you talking on the phone.''

''To Marian.'' Eyes closed, Camilla let out a long breath. ''The timing,'' she murmured, ''couldn't have been worse. I'm surprised you didn't throw me out bodily.''

''Thought about it.'' He waited until her eyes opened, met his again. ''It felt better when I sat around feeling sorry for myself. It took me a while to start considering what it's like for you. The people, the press, the protocol. It's pretty rough.''

''It's not all that bad. It's just that sometimes you have to—''

''Breathe,'' he finished.

''Yes.'' Tears swam into her eyes. ''Yes.''

''Don't do that. I can't have a rational conversation if you start dripping. Look, I mean it. Plug the dam. I've never told a woman I love her, and I'm sure as hell not going to do it for the first time when she's blubbering.''

''I'm not blubbering.'' But her voice broke on a sob as joy leaped into her. She yanked open a drawer, tugged out a lace-trimmed hankie and wiped at tears. She wanted to leap again, just leap. But this time, she knew to keep quiet. ''So, tell me.''

''I'll get to it. You're not fragile, Camilla.''

''Not as a rule, no.''

''Cordina's crown jewel. I've been catching up on some magazines,'' he said when she stared at him.

"A jewel has to have substance to keep its shine. You've got substance."

"That," she managed to say, "is the most flattering thing you've ever said to me."

"That's just because you're used to men telling you you're beautiful. And I like your family."

"My family?"

"Yeah. Your mother's an amazing woman. I like your brothers, your cousins. Still haven't quite figured out—for sure—which is which, but, I like them. And your sister's sweet." He paused. "I meant that in a good way."

"Yes." Camilla smiled a little. "She is, very sweet."

"Your aunts, uncles, they're interesting people. Admirable. I guess that's where you get it. Had some trouble with your father. But I figure if I had a daughter and some guy was... Well, it's natural for him to want to kick my ass for putting hands on what's his."

"He likes you."

"He'd like to roast me over a slow fire."

"He thinks you have potential."

Del snorted, paced, then glanced back at her. "Does he?"

"Yes. Of course if you make me unhappy, that slow fire could still be arranged. But I don't mean to pressure you."

"You're a clever girl, princess. Sharp, sexy mind. I could get past that face of yours, but your mind kept hooking me in." He gestured to the thick book on archaeology resting on her nightstand. "So you stayed interested?"

"Yes. I want to learn. I really loved working with you."

"I know."

"I find the work fascinating. Not just because of you, you know. I want to learn for me first. I needed something for myself. Something that pulled at me, from the inside. Something beyond what's expected—must be expected of me because of my position. I wanted to find my passion, and thanks to you I did. I'm making arrangements to join Dr. Lesuer on a project in France."

"Yeah, Lower Paleolithic." Del shrugged. "He's good. Hell of a teacher, too. He's got patience. I don't. It'd probably be less complicated to work with him. Then again, it'd be a shame for you to miss following through on Bardville."

She took a deep breath. "Are you suggesting that I join the project?"

"I've been thinking about outfitting a new site trailer. The old one's a dump. And I need to oversee a lot of lab work. It'd probably be practical to rent a house near the university. Maybe buy something."

The pressure in her chest was unbearable. It was wonderful. "It's understood in my family that when one of us takes a career, or makes a personal commitment, his or her official duties can be adjusted. Tell me."

"Listen, I'm going to complain every time I have to gear up in some fancy suit—and you'll probably throw my own title in my face when I do," he said, walking to her.

"Naturally."

"But I'll carry my weight on what you bring to the deal, and you'll carry yours on what I bring."

She closed her eyes briefly. "Are you asking me to ma—"

He cut her off with a quick, warning sound. "You've got some looks, don't you?" He lifted her chin and cupped her face. "Some fabulous looks. You know, I don't care how many times this face of yours is splashed over magazines. I don't care about the gossip and bull written in them, either. That kind of stuff doesn't matter to me. We know who we are."

Tears clogged her throat, shimmered in her eyes again. Nothing, nothing he might have said could have told her more clearly he believed in her. "Oh, Delaney."

"I don't have a ring for you right now."

"I don't care about that."

"I do." Funny, he thought as he lifted her hand, studied those elegant fingers, that he would feel it was important. "I want you to wear my ring." His gaze shifted to hers and held.

"If you don't want me to cry again, you'll hurry up."

"Okay, okay. Try to give a woman a little romance."

"You climbing down the palace walls is about all the romance I can take for one night. Thanks all the same."

He grinned. "I'm crazy about you. Every bit of you, but especially your smart mouth."

"That's lovely. But I could probably stand just a little more romance than that, if you can manage it."

"I love you." He took her face in his hands. This time when a tear slid down her cheek, he didn't mind. "Camilla. I love who you are. I love who we are when we're together. I love the woman who mopped my kitchen floor, and I love the woman I waltzed with tonight."

Joy soared inside her. "Both sides of that woman love all the sides of you. You make me happy."

"Marry me. Make a life with me. You won't always be comfortable, but you sure as hell won't be bored."

"I'll marry you." She touched her lips to his cheek. "And work with you." And the other. "Live with you. And love you. Always," she murmured as their lips met.

"Come back with me." He pulled her close and just held on. "We'll work out the details—whatever has to be done. I don't want to go back without you."

"Yes. I'll arrange it." She tightened her grip. "We'll arrange it."

"I'll carve out some time off—whatever we need to deal with whatever we have to deal with."

"Don't worry." Here, she thought, was her passion, her contentment and her love all wrapped in one. "We'll work it all out. When there's a question, we'll find the answer."

She rested her head on his shoulder, smiling as she felt his lips brush over her hair. The most important question, she thought, had been asked. And answered.

* * * * *

*If you enjoyed reading
Princess Camilla de Cordina's story,
then you won't want to miss the
three novels that started the series,
available for the first time in
a special 3-in-1 volume:*

CORDINA'S ROYAL FAMILY
(on sale July 2002)

containing AFFAIRE ROYALE,
COMMAND PERFORMANCE
and THE PLAYBOY PRINCE
by #1 New York Times *bestselling
author*

NORA ROBERTS

*Here's a sneak preview of the
first story in the collection,*
AFFAIRE ROYALE...

Chapter One

Swearing lightly, Reeve looked through the window at the mountains that cupped Cordina so beautifully.

Why the hell was he here? His land was thousands of miles away and waiting for his plow. Instead he was in this little fairy-tale country where the air was seductively soft and the sea was blue and close. He should never have come, Reeve told himself ruthlessly. When Armand had contacted him, he should have made his excuses.

Armand had been clever, Reeve thought grimly, very clever, to insist that he come to the hospital and see Princess Gabriella for himself. What was he going to do about her? he asked himself. What in hell was he going to do? He had his own life to start, the new one he'd chosen for himself. A man trying for a second beginning didn't have time to mix himself up in other people's problems. Hadn't that been just what he'd wanted to get away from?

His brow was furrowed in the midst of his contemplations; that was how she saw him when she opened her eyes. Brie stared into the grim, furious face, saw the smoldering blue irises, the tight mouth, and froze. What was dream and what was real? she asked herself as she braced herself. The hospital. She allowed her gaze to leave his only long enough to assure herself she was still there. Her fingers tightened on the sheets until they were white, but her voice came calmly.

"Who are you?"

Whatever else had changed about her over the years, the eyes were the same. Tawny, deep. Fascinating. Reeve kept his hands in his pockets. "I'm Reeve MacGee, a friend of your father's."

Brie relaxed a little. "Do you know me?"

"We met several years ago, Your Highness." The eyes that had fascinated him in the girl, and now in the woman, seemed to devour him. She needs something, he thought. She's groping for any handhold. "It was your sixteenth birthday. You were exquisite."

"You're American, Reeve MacGee?"

He hesitated a moment, his eyes narrowing. "Yes. How did you know?"

"Your voice." Confusion came and went in her eyes. He could almost see her grab on to that one thin thread. "I hear it in your voice. I've been there… Have I been there?"

"Yes, Your Highness."

He knew, she thought. He knew, but she could only guess. "Nothing." Tears welled up and were vanquished. She was too much her father's daughter. "Can you imagine," she began very steadily, "what it is to wake up with nothing? My life is blank pages. I have to wait for others to fill it for me. What happened to me?''

"Your Highness—"

"Must you call me that?" she demanded.

The flash of impatient spirit took him back a pace. He tried not to smile. "No," he said simply, and made himself comfortable on the edge of her bed. "What would you like to be called?"

"By my name." Brie looked down in annoyance at the bandage on her wrist. "I'm told it's Gabriella."

"You're more often known as Brie."

She was silent a moment as she struggled to find the familiarity. The blank pages remained blank. "Very well, then. Now tell me what happened to me."

"We don't have details."

"You must," she corrected, watching him. "If not all, you have some. I want them."

He studied her. Fragile, yes, but under the fragility was a core of strength. She'd have to build on it again. "Last Sunday afternoon you went out for a drive in the country. The next day, your car was found abandoned. There were calls. Ransom calls. Allegedly you'd been abducted and were being held." He didn't add what the threats had been or what would have been done to her if the ransom demands weren't met.

"Kidnapped." Brie's fingers reached out and gripped his. She saw images, shadows. A small, dark room. The smell of...kerosene and must. She remembered the nausea, the headaches. The terror came back, but little else. "It won't come clear," she murmured. "Somehow I know it's true, but there's a film I can't brush away."

"I'm no doctor." Reeve spoke in brisk tones because her fight to find herself affected him too strongly. "But I'd say not to push it. You'll remember when you're ready to remember."

"Easy to say." She released his hand. "Someone's stolen my life from me, Mr. MacGee... What's your place in this?" she demanded suddenly. "Were we lovers?"

His brow lifted. She certainly didn't beat around the bush, he mused. Nor, he thought, only half amused, did she sound too thrilled by the prospect. "As I said, you were sixteen the one and only time we met. Our fathers are old friends. They'd have been a bit annoyed if I'd seduced you."

"I see. Then why are you here?"

"Your father asked me to come. He's concerned about your security."

She glanced down at the ring on her finger. Exquisite, she thought. Then she saw her nails and frowned. That was wrong, wasn't it? She wondered. Why would she wear such a ring and not take care of her hands? Another flicker of memory taunted her. Brie closed her hands into fists as it hovered, then faded. "If my father is concerned about my security," she continued, unaware that Reeve had watched her every expression, "what is that to you?"

"I've had some experience with security. Prince Armand asked me to look out for you."

She frowned again, in a quiet, thoughtful way she had no idea was habit. "A bodyguard?" She said it in the same impatient way he had. "I don't think I'd like that."

The simple dismissal had him doing a complete reversal. He'd given up his free time, come thousands of miles, and she didn't think she'd like it. "You'll find, Your Highness, that even a princess has to do things she doesn't like. Might as well get used to it."

* * * * *

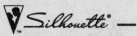

COMING NEXT MONTH